THE ROSE MASTER

REUTS PUBLICATIONS

THE
ROSE
MASTER

VALENTINA CANO

Cover design by Ashley Ruggirello
Cover art Copyright 2014 scanned-stock/TamvakisPhoto/remidica-stock/MGB-Stock/
peroni68/arca-stock on DeviantArt.com

ISBN: 978-0-9896499-7-1

REUTS Publications
www.REUTS.com

For Vicki

ONE

THE DAY I TURNED SEVENTEEN, BIRDS FELL FROM the sky. A flock of them seemed to cross an invisible line, a boundary of packed winter breezes that wrapped them up in a coat of ice, freezing whatever kernel of magic allowed them power over the air. In great chunks, like collapsing hair, they let out feathery sighs and gave in to the fall.

I was out in the courtyard, clearing a pathway through the new snow, huffing at the chill picking away at my bones. I was distracted by strange thoughts and did not see what was happening in the early dawn. Only when I began to hear the soft thuds did I turn.

Mounds of black down spotted the white courtyard. My hands flew to my mouth to cover a yelp of surprise. There were so many birds!

I hiked up my skirt, ignoring the wet hem flapping against my calves, and ran to the nearest bird to see if I could help. My footsteps crunched in the snow that piled around the indentation made by the black feathers.

A crow. A large one, with wings like melted coal, and a satin sheen to its beak that tempted my fingertips.

"Oh, you poor thing. What happened? What happened to all of you?" I looked around at the other bodies scattered in the snow. I'd never seen this before; nothing remotely like it.

I knelt beside the still figure and reached out a hand steadied by hours spent plucking larger creatures. I knew what a bird's blood looked like, smelled like, felt like under my hands. The twist of their necks, like a cracking piece of chalk, was a familiar one.

I stretched out a finger and stroked one feather. The bird let out a grey cry and scurried up, allowing its talons to grip the packed cold beneath them. It shook its head and turned its eyes toward me. I was too stunned to be frightened; all I could do was stare into its orbs—pits that shone with the knowledge of flight and wind currents, that knew rain and ice intimately.

I don't know how much time passed before the bird looked away, breaking the connection. I turned my head and saw the rest of the fallen creatures waking from their sudden slumber. One by one, they dipped their wings, seeming to churn the air around them, and lifted off once again into the London morning.

"Anne!"

My name shook through the small yard and dragged me away from the feathers and snow. I turned to Elsie, who stood by the open kitchen door, one hand holding her cap, fussing with it, pulling it and stretching it.

"Anne, come on. Lady Caldwell is calling for you."

I stood, brushed my moist hands with the inside of my skirt and trod to the open door.

"Did you see the birds?" I asked her as I passed into the bustling warmth of the kitchen.

"What birds?" Elsie pushed her cap down onto her head, tucking her light bun underneath it. She lifted a silver platter to her face and peered into its surface. "Is this on straight? Her ladyship reprimanded me yesterday for its 'unpleasant angle.' I wish I could advise her of a few 'unpleasant' things about herself."

I moved to her and waved my hand toward her head. She brought it down to my hands and I tucked in some loose threads of her hair, spreading the edge of the cap in a fan of lace.

"You didn't see the birds, then?"

"All I've seen this morning is the inside of the linen cabinet. Only the Good Lord knows why Her Rotundness needs every sheet refolded before she even dresses. She's still dawdling in her bedchamber, giving orders and dirtying teacups." She grimaced. "She wants you up there, though, so you'd better go. Wouldn't want to keep her waiting in her cozy chamber."

She pulled away from me, managing in her movement to shift the carefully placed headdress. Pushing the image of the birds away, I smiled at her turned back and groaned.

"I suppose I must." I looked out the window. "Any idea what she might want? She's always coming up with impossible requests. A few days ago, she wanted artichoke hearts. Where in the bloody hell am I supposed to get artichoke hearts in the middle of winter?"

I scrubbed my hands with a wet cloth and shrugged at my untrimmed fingernails.

"Maybe she wants to congratulate you on surviving another year." Elsie smiled at me. "How does it feel to be seventeen?"

"Well, when my fairy godmother appears and grants me all my heart's desires, I'll let you know." I lifted my head and winked at Elsie. "Perhaps I'll even meet a handsome stranger and fall in love. We'll live happily ever after in a place where there is no silver to polish."

Elsie barked out a laugh and shooed me off into the hall. As I stepped out, she turned to me again.

"Wait, what were you saying about the birds?"

"Oh, it was nothing. Forget it."

I bounced down the hall and headed for her Ladyship's rooms.

My footsteps thumped lightly on the wooden floors, their surface shining like water. I wondered what the Mistress could possibly want with me so early in the day. It couldn't be a good thing, that was certain. I passed the overstuffed sitting room with its large chairs, their bulk swallowing the room like gigantic brown mushrooms. A hideous room, but one I knew very well. I'd dusted every arm on each porcelain figurine; I'd polished the silver decanters until I thought I would die from the nausea; and I'd rubbed at the dark wood for hours, making sure the surfaces became smooth mirrors under my hands. I could have described every object and its exact placement much better than her Ladyship, and yet, nothing in there belonged to me. It never would.

I grasped the stair's banister without thought. Two steps later, I yanked my hand back.

"Damn it." I cursed under my breath. I looked around, but there was no one nearby. I listened and heard the chattering voices of the cook and two scullery maids, their piping tones vibrating through the wood around me. Lifting the edge of my clean apron, I scrubbed the finger-prints off the banister. You would think after living under the weight of domestic service my whole life, I'd be able to keep my hands to myself. I peered at the wood and smiled. No evidence of my presence remained.

With a sigh, I clutched my hands together behind my back to keep them from further insubordination, and moved with sure steps up the winding staircase. At the top, I took a moment to catch my breath before knocking on Lady Caldwell's door. It would not do to gasp out syllables in her presence; she might think it an impropriety. She seemed under the impression that if someone's heartbeat clopped along at a quicker pace than her own sedentary one, her honor was called into question. Crazy old witch.

I gathered myself, checked my uniform for untucked hems or loose strings, and then knocked once, softly.

"Enter." Her hoarse voice reached me through the coffin-like door. I rolled my eyes and opened it.

"Anne, it's very kind of you to grace me with your presence. I only asked for you half an hour ago."

I curtsied. "I beg your pardon, your Ladyship. I was delayed."

"When I ask for something, it must be brought at once. You should know better, Anne."

"Yes, your Ladyship." I curtsied again, trying to keep from toppling over. I'd never been much good at curtsying.

A long moment of silence followed. Lady Caldwell fussed with her powders and creams, opening and closing jars that promised much more than they could ever grant. Her size always amazed me, no matter how many years I'd been coming in and out of her presence. She was a large woman, every aspect of her multiplied, from her chin to the creases in her elbows, all of them doubled, sometimes tripled. It didn't help that her fashion sense hadn't evolved along with her bulge.

My leg itched. How much longer did she want to hold me in suspense? I had the whole china cabinet to dust, along with a multitude of other pointless duties that just *had* to be performed every day. God forbid a pillow went without fluffing.

Finally, she put her creams down and inhaled. "You turned seventeen today." It was not a question. Her Ladyship never deigned to ask questions.

"Yes, your Ladyship."

"Good. Now, Anne, you have been in my household a long time, at least ten years, and in that time I have seen you grow into a capable youth, someone who has the makings of a competent housekeeper. As you well know, this house has many servants who are older and who have a better chance of reaching that position before you do." She looked at me. "You also know how much I appreciated your mother's company when she was my personal maid, and it's because of her that I called you in here today. I feel I have a better opportunity for you."

I kept silent and waited. This was certainly unusual.

After rummaging through her drawers, she pulled out a letter. "I've recently received a note from a distant relative, someone of whom I have little recollection, but who seems to remember me well enough to have sent me this by post. It appears his household, Rosewood Manor, is in need of a maid, someone who does not need to be trained in the managing of every-day tasks and who has potential to become a leader. I've been asked to recommend someone discreet, obedient, disciplined, and self-sufficient. The work would involve a bit more than what you are required in my service because it is a smaller staff, but for that same reason, you would have an almost sure place at the head of the household. I have sent word to your father at Exter House, and he has agreed with my decision. I have full confidence you are the appropriate person, having come from sturdy parents with impressive references. Your father's employer calls him his 'most attentive valet,' a high compliment indeed, from someone who's had as many as Lord Exter."

The news she'd contacted my father shocked me more than her previous words. I hadn't seen him in about a year, what with Lord Exter going off on one voyage after another, always dragging my only parent along.

Lady Caldwell's voice brought me back to attention: "I have notified Rosewood Manor of your imminent arrival."

Imminent arrival? "Pardon me, madam, but when will I be departing?"

"Why, in two day's time. I thought I mentioned that. Now . . ."

Her voice faded, coming in and out, grazing me like a beam from a lighthouse. At first, all I could feel was panic. I'd been raised between the walls of this place—cold ones, to be sure, but the only ones I knew. A house I'd grown to like, if not love. But I now saw the silliness I'd lived under, thinking myself safe, not realizing I was expendable, a rug that could be rolled up and shipped somewhere else.

Her voice flooded in. "So make sure you are prepared to depart. It is a long journey. Plan to spend many uncomfortable hours on a coach."

"A coach, your Ladyship?" I was stunned even further.

"Yes, it seems your new employer has eccentric ways of going about things, and transporting a new maid in a personal coach is just one of them. I expect, of course, for you to be on exemplary behavior. I will not have any relative of mine, however distant, suffering under my recommendation."

"I would never dream of putting your Ladyship in that position."

She cleared her throat. "Good. Now that this business is settled, you may go back to work."

"Yes, your Ladyship." I curtsied again and turned. I opened the door and stepped into the dark corridor, walking toward a corner in a more secluded part of the second story. I blinked back hot tears and clenched my fists, focusing my attention on the cuts my fingernails were molding into my palms.

It all seemed so sudden. In two days time, I'd be leaving—forever.

A wave of fear washed over and away from me, leaving me limp. Slowly, I got my breathing back to normal; after all, there was nothing I could do. My hands stopped shaking and, with a pair of newly dried eyes, I climbed down the staircase. My hands were gripped behind my back.

TWO

ELSIE YANKED MY ARM TOWARD HER. "WHAT DO you mean you've been dismissed?" Her large blue eyes became even larger on her paling face.

I shrugged. "Her Ladyship no longer needs me in her household. She's shipping me off to some relative's home. Some place called Rosewood Manor."

"She's not really dismissing you, then. She's lending you out for a while. I'm sure she'll want you back." Elsie's voice sounded breathless and twittering from nerves. The cook, Mary, snorted behind us. I looked at her thick hands, the color and texture of rough leather, spilling chicken giblets onto the chopping board. I grimaced and thanked the Lord my days as a kitchen maid were long behind me.

"She might as well be kicking you off into the street, child. Rosewood is in the middle of nowhere, trees surrounding it on four sides, not a soul nearby. Not a pleasant place. Not when you've lived in the city all your life."

"How do you know all that? Have you ever seen it?" I asked.

"Not me, but my husband had an acquaintance who worked there, back when old Lord Grey ruled the home. He used to complain about the silence, said it was worse than the cold. And it does get cold up there. I don't know if Lord Grey still lives, but I'm sure he had children who still own the manor."

"Lady Caldwell said they were relations."

Mary smiled and poured chopped onions into a pan. "Wouldn't surprise me. These lords and ladies are always tied to each other, what with marrying cousins off to one another and all that."

"Ugh!" Elsie cried.

"Yes, it's not nice to think of, but they wouldn't want the blood-lines polluted with the likes of us, now would they?" She chuckled, a harsh sound. I turned to Elsie, who still had my arm clutched inside her moist palm. With a pang, I realized that I would be leaving her behind in a few days—the person I could very well call my sister; the only family I could truly think of as mine. I turned my head, trying to keep the rebellious tears from trickling out.

"The coach will be here in two days to take me to Rosewood."

Elsie gasped and released my arm, surprising me with the force of her recoil. "That's too soon." She blinked and clutched at her neck, as if I'd reached out and wrapped my hands around its girth.

"There's nothing to be done, my father has already agreed. I have to go."

She shook her head, shock bright in her eyes, and ran out of the room. I sighed. She'd calm down on her own. It wasn't for nothing I'd shared a room with her for ten years.

"Don't you have things to do, Anne?" Mary said.

I blinked out of my thoughts and shook my hands in frustration. "Yes. Yes, of course I do."

I headed to the blasted china cabinet in the dining room, with its cubbyholes that sustained whole populations of dust balls and its gleaming plates in perfect rows, like a grinning mouth. I had my cloth prepared—a soft flannel with a slightly moist side to pick up the grains of dust and dirt—gripped the first plate with both hands, and brought it down toward my body. The engraved, golden letter "C" seemed to mock me with its delicacy.

What is the matter with me today? It's a plate, not a scheming oracle.

I began the tedious work, moving with the careful monotony of well-rehearsed steps, my mind unwinding as I brushed cup after cup, plate after plate. Maybe it wouldn't be so bad. After all, hadn't I been complaining about Lady Caldwell's manias just a half-hour ago? I would never have to straighten up her row of collectible porcelain again, the slippery figures tinkling even in my dreams.

It would be a change. I would miss Elsie, of course. How could I not? Even the thought of abandoning her threatened to set me crying, but . . .

But nothing, I told myself in stern tones. Nothing to be done about the whole thing. Besides, I'd never seen the countryside, and Rosewood Manor sounded like a peaceful place. As I lay a teacup back into its shelf, I smiled. It might not be so terrible.

After supper had been served for Lord and Lady Caldwell, the rest of us sat down to a quick meal before being rung back to provide nightcaps and, for her Ladyship, her usual cup of peppermint tea. We alternated between each other on that particular task, and tonight, the sword fell on my head. I groaned as I poured hot water on the powdery leaves, the smell floating up to me in a cloud of crispness, green, and cold; what I imagined a snow-covered pine tree would taste like. Not that I went around chewing pine needles.

Gripping the silver tray in two less-than-steady hands, I trailed back up the long staircase for what felt like the millionth time that day. The teacup scraped against its plate, setting my teeth on edge, but I finally made it to Lady Caldwell's bedchamber. I cradled the tray against my side and released one hand to knock on the door, but as I brushed my knuckle to the wood, I caught movement off to my left. Curiosity was a fault of mine. A pretty large one, as it turned out.

The dim light from the scarab-like sconces did not allow a clear view of what had flickered past the corner of my eye. The shadows the pale lights drew forth obscured everything not directly under them. I knelt and placed the tray on the floor.

Walking forward with silence draped around me, I stepped toward the motion. I gasped as I saw more flickering, silver strands dancing in the moonlight pouring from one of the windows.

On the half-frozen pane were dozens of moths, their muslin wings extended in paused flight, their impassive faces staring at me. I'd never seen so many before, their spun sugar bodies covering every inch of the glass. I raised my hands slowly, placing my palms against the window, and, for an instant, I held a sheet of moths. Then the little bodies fell, and I jerked back. My heart stabbed its beats through my ribs, creating havoc with my breath. Surprise was quickly replaced with a gritty fear that refused to be brushed away. First the birds, and now the moths! There had to be something wrong in the city today; these could not be random events.

A sudden exhaustion dropped onto me. Every muscle jerked, and my every bone ached with hollow moans. My eyelids drooped, and I found I could hardly move.

I needed to get that tea to Lady Caldwell, but holding the tray between my hands did not seem like a good idea at the moment. I'd end up with peppermint-soaked stockings and one more tea set deducted from my pay. I shook my hands out, trying to get the blood that seemed to have deserted them moving, coaxing it back into circulation.

"I'm all right," I said under my breath.

"Anne, is that you?" Elsie's voice reached me from the staircase. Oh, thank God.

"Yes, it's me. Elsie, can you help me a bit? I don't seem to be feeling too well." Within seconds she was beside me, peering into my face under one of the lamps.

"You look horrible!"

"Thanks. I try."

"No, I mean, really. What happened?"

I shook my head and shrugged. "I don't know. One minute I was fine and the next, I thought I'd faint." My hands still trembled a bit against my thighs.

"What were you doing up here, anyway?" she asked.

I pointed to the tray, still lying accusingly on the floor where I'd left it. "I was bringing the tea. It was my turn tonight." As I spoke, a weight seemed to lift off my chest and breathing became easier. My muscles relaxed, once again plump with air.

"Oh, that's better," I exhaled.

Elsie eyed me. "I'll take Lady Caldwell her damn tea. You just wait here. Don't go down the stairs by yourself, just in case."

I nodded as she turned and picked up the tea set in her sure grip. She knocked once and entered. I leant my back against the ridiculous wallpaper, an avalanche of flowers and manic birds, and took steady breaths, enjoying my newfound calmness. A few minutes later, I heard the click of a door closing.

"All right, let's go." Elsie guided me to the staircase.

"I'm just tired, not at death's door."

"Could have fooled me," she snapped.

I bit my lip and kept quiet as we trod down to the first floor. She led me to our room.

"I'll go pick up the tray, don't worry. Just lie down and see if you can sleep. Do you want me to bring you anything, some water, maybe?"

"No. Thanks, Elsie." I held her gaze and smiled. "You saved an innocent cup and saucer from sure extermination."

She chuckled. "It's a good thing you had enough sense to set it down."

I didn't tell her the real reason why I'd abandoned it to the floor. I just didn't have the strength for it, and I wasn't sure she'd believe me even if I did. I wasn't sure I believed it myself.

She took one more look at me and, after assuring herself I wasn't going to expire in the next few minutes, left. I seriously considered falling into my bed fully clothed, but decided against it. No point in soiling the bedsheets.

I unpinned my cap, untied my apron and my dress, and slid off my petticoats and shoes. I threw on my nightdress and dug into my coverlet, the chill of our room having seeped into it enough for me to shiver. I sighed and closed my eyes.

Right before slumber took me, I saw the moths once again, their gentle bodies buzzing under my palms.

THREE

THE NEXT DAY HARDLY LEFT AN IMPRINT ON ME. It passed in a fog of dust, cleaning vinegar, wet rags, and wood wax.

If I had expected it to be marked somehow, separated from the rest, I would have been wrong. My impending departure seemed to affect no one except Elsie, who was still morose, but had at least managed to keep her tears in check. She'd alluded to the previous night's brief spell of sickness, but I'd waved her away with a feather duster, brandishing its fluff like a sword. I didn't feel sick.

My mind kept fiddling with what little I knew about my new position. I knew nothing of my employer, except possibly his family's name, and I had a vague idea of what my duties would consist of, but I was sure a country home, even a manor, was run in a different style than a city one. Her Ladyship had said it would be a similar type of position, so at least I could expect the basic indignities of service life: the emptying of chamber pots, the yanking of moist bedsheets, the waxing of filthy floors . . . as long as I did not have to take on any of the scullery maid's duties, I would be fine. I had been through that particular type of work years ago, when my mother had first brought me to be trained in household service.

Her Ladyship was right. I did come from a long line of maids and gardeners, coach drivers and stable keepers, with the odd butler or housekeeper thrown in. My family's blood had lived alongside some of the wealthiest and most influential people of London—small comfort when you had to carry yet another night's worth of human waste down endless stairs.

My mother had served Lady Caldwell for years before she had met and married my father, so she had been in good standing to ask for my admittance to the household. I did not remember much about my mother. She'd died when I was still too young to engrave her features in memory's mold. And I barely saw my father, even after my mother died. Only on Sundays, at church, could we sometimes greet each other, but for too many months out of the year, he traveled with his employer. He'd been Lord Exter's valet for years, a toothy man who laughed like a cat battling a hairball.

My father, Henry, was a man who valued propriety above all else. It wasn't surprising, really, since his parents had both been crucial members of Exter House's staff. He'd been raised watching his mother choose to serve her employer before feeding her own child, and yet he held no resentment for the life he was born into. He enjoyed his duties, such as they were, and even now, liked nothing better than to earn Lord Exter's curt nod of approval. Whenever I was in doubt of anything, his voice was the one I heard, pointing me to where my duties lay.

My mother, Agnes, had been a different creature altogether. I'd painted a blurred portrait of her as someone full of anxious fire from what Mary had told me over the years. She'd had ambition for herself, which, for a servant, and a female one at that, was not the healthiest of attitudes to possess. She'd chafed under the rules that made little sense to her, yet she'd had no power to change them. Her intelligence and knack for taking command of situations had earned her a place next to Lady Caldwell, but still, before she became ill, she had begun to yearn for more, like a horse tugging at the reins. Mary had known her well and always answered whatever questions I might have about her, but it wasn't the same. I missed her, though I never really knew her.

My father had met my mother in a celebration of something or other, when the two households (and many more) had come together for a few days of reveling. My parents had begun exchanging letters as frequently as work had allowed and, after a few years, had decided marriage would not be a bad idea. They'd managed to conceive me by some manner of miraculous juggling that I've never cared to investigate further, but their lives never truly joined as normal husband and wife. It was not possible, not with them living in different households. Their employers, of course, did not find it convenient to allow one of them to leave so they could be together. My father had bowed to Lord Exter's wishes without too much fuss and had left my mother to care for me at Caldwell House while he fetched cuff links and straightened bow ties.

Many servants went through that, though. I might even go through that when I decided to marry and have a family of my own, but still, the thought of it left me cold.

When my mother died, I was taken in by Mary, who was an interesting version of motherhood. She possessed little patience in general, even less for children, and she'd already had Elsie to care for by the time I ended up motherless. I was grateful, however, for even her rough care and lack of demonstrative affection. If it weren't for her, I don't know what would have happened to me, since I doubted Lord Exter would have welcomed my four-year-old presence into his orderly household. I wasn't too sure my father would have either, for that matter. In his eyes, I would have disturbed the proper order of things.

It had taken a bit to accustom myself to Mary, but I'd learned one very important trait from her: self-sufficiency. She was never one to coddle.

By the time I was five, I could kill and pluck a chicken on my own, and I could chop carrots at a good clip without slicing off any fingers. I'd hated all of it, though. I could not stand the smell of raw meat, and I could have committed crimes after chopping bowl after bowl of walnuts. The kitchen was not for me. I'd loved to watch Elsie, though, as she and Mary prepared dishes and meals for entire banquets. Getting to sneak a treat when they weren't looking wasn't too awful, either.

When I became old enough to work as a parlor maid, I'd gladly clasped the broom and set out for the dusty trenches. I was good at it, and as much as I complained, I liked the way an object seemed to reemerge from a film of powder. All I could wish for in my new position was that whatever my employer had in mind for me did not involve boiling pots.

The more I thought of my impending departure, the more my heart ached at leaving Elsie. We'd been inseparable from the day we'd met, two motherless girls chattering late into the night. I knew there was only one Elsie, but would there be anyone even remotely like her at Rosewood

Manor? Would there be anyone with whom I could laugh and speak in earnest?

I could only hope so.

When night finally came and we tucked in to a hasty supper, the butler, Mr. Easton, coughed softly and looked down the table. He cleared his throat and everyone turned to face him, some still chewing.

"I have been notified that one of us will be departing tomorrow morning to a new position." He looked at me with his warm, blue eyes. "Although we will miss her, I, for one, wish Anne the best in her new home, and I am convinced she will make a wonderful addition to their staff." He nodded toward me and sipped his water.

"Thank you, Mr. Easton," I said.

The conversation picked up again, the latest news overriding the rather tame announcement. They were used to servants leaving, either from being dismissed or by their own volition, and did not find it the least bit strange to say so simple a goodbye to someone they could very well never see again.

I picked at my food. My stomach churned at the thought that it'd be the last night I'd spend around that table. Elsie reached her hand under the tablecloth and clasped my free one. I turned to her and gave her a pale smile.

The following morning was a rare one, the type that forced people into the street, blinking in the glare of the sudden, unfamiliar sun. I found it a blaring irony that my last day in London should have been marked by such beauty, as if the city rejoiced at my leaving it. Of course, that was utter nonsense. The city couldn't have cared less if I got run over by a drunken carriage.

I dressed with care, picking among the few items that did not comprise my former uniform. I looked at one of the two dresses I possessed (and the only one without holes), holding it up to my face in the mirror, and grimaced. Neither the fabric, nor the anemic color of milky tea complemented my already pale skin. My dark eyes and hair helped, but not much.

With an exasperated sigh, I stepped into the dress, almost falling over as my foot caught in the ragged hem, and tied the laces. It was a snug fit. I'd grown since I'd bought it. How many months ago had that been? At least a year, if not longer, and I was still dumbfounded at my color choice. What had I been thinking? Probably that I'd rather have a pale, simple dress to one of those frilled monstrosities women seemed to love.

I buttoned what needed to be buttoned and tucked and flattened and pulled until the mirror held up a presentable image. I pinned my hair in a quick bun and grabbed my bonnet and traveling bag, the same one that had carried my childhood clothes years before. As I grasped the bag's smooth handle, the memory of a warm touch on my free hand made me stop. My mother had guided me into Caldwell House. I shrugged off the ache I felt. No one would guide me out.

The hall was deserted and the gleaming wood, like liquid chocolate, blinked all around me. I could have paused to say my goodbyes to the familiar rooms, but I did not.

I walked to the kitchen where voices poured out with the smell of fresh herbs. Voices I'd heard for most of my life, ones I could recognize in any context, any situation, their inflections as unique as the throats that contained them. I closed my eyes and breathed.

I pushed the door open and the voices quieted. Mary and Elsie stared back at me, the older woman smiling, while my best friend, my sister, attempted to hold back tears unsuccessfully. I felt my voice catch in my throat, and I cleared it with a rough cough.

"I think the coach is here."

"Well, child," Mary said, coming up to me. "I wish you a safe trip. You'll be fine, Anne. Don't you worry." She kissed my forehead with her dry lips and smiled again. I thought I caught a glimmer of tears in her eyes.

Elsie, by then, was sopping wet and sniffling. I walked up to her and enveloped her in my arms, causing further sobs to rack her frame. I hummed an old song in her ear—one of our favorites—brushing her back like a mother soothing a child. My own tears stained her uniform, and I knew I couldn't wait much longer. If I did, I'd never leave.

"I have to go, Elsie," I whispered.

She gripped me harder for an instant, then released me. "I know."

"It's not like I'm going away to America. I won't be that far from here." Smiling, I pulled a lock of her hair back from her face.

"You won't forget me?" she asked.

"What a silly question! Never. Write to me if you get a chance."

She nodded.

I blew her a kiss, picked up my bag, and walked to the door.

"I'll walk you to the coach," Elsie said.

"No, I think it's best if I go on my own. No need to make it harder on both of us." With a last smile that most likely looked more like a grimace, I left the kitchen.

Tears spilled down, and I brushed at them in fury.

"Pull yourself together, Anne. You're an adult," I chided myself. "What would Father say?"

Mr. Easton was there by the front door.

"Good morning, Anne," he said.

"Good morning," I managed to squeak out.

"The carriage is waiting."

"Good."

He opened the door and I stepped past him into the sunlight. Mr. Easton grasped my shoulder in his gentle hand.

"Take care of yourself, Anne."

"I will, sir."

He smiled and nodded, releasing me into the world.

FOUR

I'D NEVER RIDDEN IN A COACH BEFORE, HAVING depended on my own not-always-solid feet for transport, so when the driver helped me up the contraption in front of me, I had no idea what to expect.

The seats were a dark purple and soft to the touch. The windows were large. I asked if I could open at least one of them, so I could see the change of scenery. I wanted to see what I naively imagined as a clear borderline between London's edge and the rest of the country. I was not sure what I expected, a pathway made of smoke, a line of flaming torches, certainly not what I did see: a wide road turning into a dirt ribbon, the jostle of the carriage the only indication we'd left the city.

I was smiling despite myself, though, waving at every tree we passed, creatures that were almost mythological in stony London. I stuck my head out the window and breathed deeply. The driver turned to me and gave a slight frown, so I tucked back inside and settled myself on the seat.

He was a peculiar man, the driver. He had such a look of fright in his pale eyes that I wasn't sure he'd last the whole trip. His words were clipped, and his voice was so low I had to stare at his lips to understand the few words he spoke. I could not comprehend why he was so perturbed. I was not an imposing being; there was no astounding beauty to my face that might have earned me the hesitant looks and slight flinches I saw. I shrugged as I thought about it and hoped he would be more relaxed when we stopped around midday, since I couldn't very well speak to him from inside the carriage. I would have had to scream, and I assumed that would give the man an apoplexy.

But when the time came to stop at a nearby inn for a quick meal, I found his attitude to have worsened, if anything. He paid for our meals, a pleasant surprise, but he winced when I thanked him, as if I had slapped him with my voice. So I bit my tongue and ate my vegetable stew in silence.

Back on the road, I found myself lulled despite the excitement of the day and the expectation of reaching Rosewood Manor. Even my thoughts of Elsie grew a film of sleep over them. I'd never smelled air as emerald green as that which reached my nose from the open window. It was all so different from the sooty, squirming, London life I was accustomed to. Just to sit idle for hours at a time, without anything to occupy my hands, was a new experience.

The sun stroked my face with warmth that all but commanded my eyelids to waver. As the sun sang its lullaby to my senses, my mind stilled, and I stopped my internal pacing, surrendering to sleep.

I was awakened by a slight chill. I felt dizzy and my head was too heavy to lift, as it had invariably felt the few times in my life I'd been allowed an afternoon nap. My neck was stiff from the odd position I'd slept in and it creaked like an old, angry door as I moved it from side to side.

The sun was setting. It looked large, important against the white fields, not like the shadow it was in London, always obscured by one building or another.

At the next inn, the driver decided to stop. He eased me down, but when I opened my mouth to thank him, he pulled away and scurried off into the brick building. I raised my hands in frustration and followed him in.

The place was cozy, if a bit shabby, with tables that wobbled and wine stains on the floor, but the smell of meat, dark and velvet, made me forgive any lack of beauty.

I sat down on an empty chair and waited for the driver to return. When he did, he sat down across from me and placed two mugs between us. I peered into mine, the greasy handle sliding between my fingers. I sniffed, but it had no scent. Sipping, I realized it was just water and not the cleanest I'd ever had, with an aftertaste that could only be described as the taste of dust. I was thirsty, so I drank it anyway. As I swallowed, I peered at the man, the mug creating a horizon across his face. He was not looking at me or at anything, his gaze caught by the uneven table boards.

"Sir, how much longer do we have until the manor?" I realized as I spoke that I didn't even know his name.

"A few more hours, miss." He did not look at me.

"Are we continuing on tonight, or are we stopping here?"

"It's too dark. We'll stop here, miss."

I had trouble understanding him. I was about to ask him a bit about Rosewood Manor when a maid brought our plates. Potatoes and meat. Not fancy, but filling and warm. In between bites, I gazed at the driver, who picked at his food, cutting smaller and smaller pieces and then abandoning the plate altogether.

"Sir, I'm sorry, I don't recall if you told me your name. I dislike not knowing who I am speaking with." I smiled and tried to look as reassuring as possible.

"Peter Keery, miss."

"Well, Mr. Keery, I must admit I am rather curious about my employer. No one at Caldwell House knew about him. Is it still Lord Grey?"

"Lord Grey's son, miss." He fidgeted.

"Oh."

"I'm sorry, miss, would it be improper to ask you to excuse me? I'm awfully tired."

I placed my fork down. "Of course."

He stood. "Your room is number sixteen, the third at the top of the landing. Here is the key." He scraped it across the table. "We'll leave early tomorrow morning, miss."

I nodded. I opened my mouth to wish him goodnight, but he had already disappeared.

FIVE

WE DEPARTED AHEAD OF THE DAWN. MR. KEERY appeared as hesitant as the day before, and I was too tired to persevere in opening him up like a clamshell. Let him keep quiet if he pleased; I'd soon have other things with which to concern myself. It was cooler than the previous morning, enough for me to shut the window in an attempt to keep my blood from growing icy spikes.

I chafed against the boredom of the ride (made terrible without the pleasure of the scenery), so I rummaged through my bag and brought out my Bible—small and scuffed, but bearing my initials in crimson thread on the cover. It had been a present from my father years before, and I'd learned to thumb through it at odd moments. My father always felt closer when I held it, regardless of where in the world he might be roaming. All the things I missed after so many months of barely any contact would come into my head—his thin smile, his sure hands, the way he'd nod as I recounted my daily life at Caldwell House. I didn't even have an address to be able to write to him. And for his part, although he knew of my new position, he would not have time in the midst of the whirlwind that was Lord Exter's life to send me even the simplest of notes.

I sighed, flipped at random through the onionskin pages, and read the first passage my eyes landed on.

I nodded at the words and sighed at their musical syllables. Quite pretty. I wondered why my parents hadn't insisted on my Christian upbringing, as I hadn't ever laid a finger on a Bible until my mother passed away. She hadn't been opposed, exactly, but she'd never given it the importance my father thought it deserved. Or, at least, that's what I'd heard from Mary. My father, on the other hand, was the most devout man I'd ever met. He could recite entire passages from memory without a single stumble. He'd tried, in his way, to teach me about faith, but it was still confusing to me, all the different stories with all their different versions, all the hidden meanings tucked like seeds in the folds of the sentences. Church hadn't helped much either. Lady Caldwell had had a strict rule about her employees attending Sunday services, so I'd been taken every week for the past ten years. Still, the sermons were convoluted; sounds that enticed murmurs from the congregation, but that had nothing to say to my thirsty mind. I was indifferent to religion, and I didn't want to be.

Perhaps I would have the opportunity to ask my questions at whichever church I'd be attending at my new home. Maybe a country church would provide the relaxed atmosphere I needed to embrace the meaning of the book I held in my hands.

I kissed it, as I'd been taught to do, and tucked it back into my travel bag. I settled back in the seat, untying my bonnet, and allowed my thoughts to spread.

The first sign that we were nearing our destination came in through the small slit of window I'd left open—the scent of roses. I couldn't believe it at first. It trickled in and filled the coach with its thick odor. I flung the rest of the window open and was grasped by the full madness of the flowers. I inhaled and laughed as the perfume filled my lungs, my chest cavity, my stomach.

I yelled up at Mr. Keery: "We are getting close, right, sir?"

"Yes, miss, we are almost there."

I took out my small mirror and inspected my hair, pulling and tucking as needed until I could easily fit its brown mass under the bonnet. I caught my reflection, smiling, wide eyes glittering in the perfumed air.

"We're almost there," I told the girl in the mirror. As I peered into my face (one that didn't brim over with beauty, but which was pretty enough), a vague hope filled my head. Perhaps there might even be someone interesting at Rosewood, someone with whom I could settle down into a quiet life. I had turned seventeen, after all.

There was a sudden jolt as the coach came to an abrupt stop. I reached out my hands to steady myself and looked out. Mr. Keery was swinging the reins and urging the halted horses to continue, but they whinnied and pulled their ears back.

"What's wrong with the horses?" I asked.

"Just a bit spooked, miss. Don't trouble yourself."

The snorts and stomps told me they were more than "a bit spooked." I opened the door and climbed down with care onto the dirt road that wound through the snow.

"Miss, please, you'll catch cold."

I ignored him and walked up to the animals, laying my hands on the muscular side of the one closest to me. Their skin visibly twitched without pause.

"These animals are terrified!" I told Mr. Keery. "Look at the foam in their mouths!" I moved to face the creatures and began a stream of comforting words, pouring vowels into the two sets of ears before me. I did not say anything in particular, just the nonsense a mother would say to a slumbering child to keep the dark wings of nightmares away, but it seemed to soothe the poor beasts. I extended my arms and wrapped them around the horses, pulling them toward my body so that I had their heaving chests against my sides. I'd done this countless times with frightened fowl, and even once or twice with Elsie after she'd had a nightmare, but never with any creature this large.

I felt their muscles unknotting themselves, and the foam slowly stopped spewing from their mouths. My breathing had also slowed, and I suddenly felt exhausted. I could have fallen right to the ground if not for the warm bodies I still held. I waited for the dizziness to pass, wondering if there was something wrong with me. Two fainting spells in a single week.

The wave of relief soon came and I walked away from the horses. But as soon as I withdrew my hands, they began their snorting again, this time even louder and more frantic.

"Are you all right, miss? You look terribly pale," Mr. Keery said.

"I'm fine, but these horses . . ."

"They quieted down with you."

I nodded. With a smile, I took the reins from his hands.

"Miss?"

"If I walk in front of them for a bit, maybe they'll get back to normal." Before he could say anything, I pulled the reins and took a step forward. With a last set of whinnying, the horses began moving once more.

The pathway became more difficult to traverse, with stones that had to be chucked and snow in thick mounds that made me wince as the wheels crunched through them.

I could not help gazing around me in awe.

I'd never seen such whiteness, and, in all honesty, I felt unnerved; a trickle of hot fear tickled down my arms and legs. There were no bird cries of any sort; the only sound was the muffled hooves of the steaming beasts behind me. With a start, I realized why the path was so difficult to move through: it was untrodden. No one had passed that way since the last snowfall, at least two days ago. No one had entered or left the vicinity of Rosewood Manor.

I turned my head to Mr. Keery, who walked next to the horses, his eyes never straying too far from his feet. In the harsh and icy daylight, he looked even worse than the day before. His complexion would have been ruddy in better conditions, but at the moment, he looked like a slab of cold cheese, pockmarked and sagging. Once in a while, he muttered to himself in a string of sounds I could not catch. He grimaced and jerked under the weight of his own words.

I shivered, turning my eyes back to the road. The horses had not stopped again, and we were making good time. By my calculations (which could have been off by a whole day for all I knew of countryside traveling), we would be at the manor in an hour or so. I hoped the people at Rosewood had had the sense to set water boiling for baths, because I did not want to meet my employer with streaks of salt decorating my hems.

Half an hour later, the trees seemed to have bowed and scurried apart. A narrow track opened up underneath our feet.

"We're near." Mr. Keery's voice made me jump after the thin crust of silence that had covered us for so long.

The trees somehow looked darker, more imposing, yet crooked and hunchbacked, their bare arms stretched in supplication.

Stop that, I told myself. *They are just ordinary trees.*

"Do you think we can get back on the coach now? I would hate to arrive like this at the manor." He looked at me as if he'd never seen me before. His mouth hung loose, an empty basket of bones and teeth. He took a deep breath and blinked.

"Oh, miss, I'm sorry, did you say something?"

I repeated my question and he eyed the horses.

"I doubt it, miss. These horses have never been outside Lord Grey's grounds, so they are frightened. Rightly so."

"They've never left the grounds? But surely your master has to run errands or the like."

He shook his head. "No, miss, we are pretty isolated."

I was starting to see that. The air was much cooler between the trees that fringed the road. Why would anyone choose to live here? Especially with the wealth Lord Grey apparently had? It made little sense.

The smell of roses lingered in the air, playing with the chilled breezes, floating toward and away from us as it chose. I had grown almost used to it.

Without fanfare, we maneuvered through an exhausted-looking, thick pair of trees and rounded on Rosewood Manor. My breath hitched in my lungs. The size of the place! It had at least four wings, chiseled columns, and a stone facade that was as frightening as it was sturdy. Yet nothing looked taken care of. Everything had a sheen of neglect that changed what could have been a beautiful place into a disquieting image that loomed before me as we walked.

And then, there were the roses. There's never been a more appropriate name for a place than the name which crowned that manor. On either side, almost leading us, were rose bushes, their red flowers pooling petals on the snow like drops of blood. Underneath every window on the still distant house, I could spot more roses, all red and large. All perfectly timed and blooming in fragrant defiance of winter.

We stepped onto the final path which led straight to the front door and my knees buckled under the cloak of perfume that enveloped me. I hadn't realized how affected I'd been. My head spun as if I'd had too much wine.

Mr. Keery gripped my arm to keep me upright.

"Welcome to Rosewood Manor," he said.

SIX

THEY MUST HAVE KNOWN WE WERE ARRIVING that day, and yet no one was at the door to receive us. I stood on the steps leading up to the entrance, trying to brush the winter off my clothes, unsure what I should do. I saw Mr. Keery grab the coach's reins and start pulling the horses toward where I assumed the stables lay.

"Wait, sir, what am I supposed to do?"

He looked at me with the same shaken eyes. "Why, miss, go in."

"Just go in? Through the front door?" The thought of stepping onto what I was certain would be spotless, gleaming floors sent my heart pounding. My shoes were so crusted over in muddied snow they could have kept walking on their own. My father's face would have paled in horror at my even considering such a thing.

Mr. Keery sniffed. "We don't stand on too much ceremony here. Just go in. I'm sure there'll be someone in the kitchen." He turned and dragged his feet down a side path.

Bloody hell. I glanced around, but there was no one. It seemed I had no choice. Taking a deep breath, I broke every rule I'd ever been taught. I gripped the freezing doorknob and opened the door. The glare off the snow behind me made it difficult to see inside. I had to blink and wait as my eyes decided to get back to work. They cleared by slow degrees, revealing a strange room. It was large and almost empty, with only a chandelier that looked like a bouquet of dead branches, and a couple of the meanest-looking wooden benches I'd ever seen. Highly unusual furnishings for the day and age, when everything tended to be swaddled in silks and damasks, with ornaments teetering on crowded side tables.

And the cold. I turned to make sure I'd closed the door behind me when I realized just how much I was trembling. It was colder inside than outside! But it was a different version of cold, one that felt heavy in the air, like an endless shriek.

I had expected my footsteps to echo along the stone floors, but they hardly dented the silence. The kitchen. Where was the kitchen? I moved across the floor until I saw two other doors, both closed and peering at me while I stood hesitating between them. I chose the one on my left and opened it.

"Well, you must be Anne," a voice said.

I stepped into the room and saw two women sitting around a stained and bruised table. One was young, about my age, with a head of flaming hair that was not tucked or pinned in any noticeable manner. Her features were too regular to be called pretty, but she had a bright look about her that set me at ease.

The other woman was a different matter. She was middle-aged and showed it, her face grooved as if someone had dragged fork tines over it while she slept. She was the one who'd spoken.

"Yes, ma'am, I am Anne." I curtsied. She was probably the house-keeper, so I'd better be on my best behavior.

To my surprise, she laughed. "There's no need to go bending your knees around here, except maybe in front of the master."

I found my voice. "Yes, ma'am."

The red-haired woman spoke up. "I'm Theodora. Isn't that just horrid? I think so. Anyway, everyone calls me Dora, and this handsome place is my domain." She winked at me, gesturing with her arms to the dilapidated kitchen around us. It was warmer, both in temperature and atmosphere, than the front parlor, but the dankness still seeped in through the gap under the door. The kitchen was passably clean, though I could see specks of dust floating in the air. I stared at some of the copper pots hanging like gilded snails off the walls and saw the white film of dust that had accumulated on them. Did they not use the pots?

"And I am Ms. Simple, the housekeeper." She grimaced at the title and gave me a small smile. "You have been hired, as I'm sure you know, to be the parlor maid. Since you come from Lady Caldwell's household, I doubt I need to go pointing out your duties?"

I swallowed. "I know my duties, ma'am. Should I ask one of the other girls to show me the different rooms? I fear I'll get lost if I attempt it on my own."

The two women eyed each other. Ms. Simple sighed. "Anne, there are no other girls. It's just the two of us and the coachman. The master doesn't even keep a manservant."

My hands fluttered and clenched on my skirt. "But surely I'm not expected to maintain the entire manor on my own! It's impossible!"

"Don't upset yourself. We'd never expect that kind of sacrifice from you. No, we only use a small section of the place. Many of the rooms, as you will see, are locked. Just do what you can, and the rest, leave. We all manage. Dora here did not know how to boil an egg a month ago, but necessity is the best teacher."

"And the cook, what happened to her?"

Dora's blue eyes turned to me. "She left."

"Why?"

Ms. Simple shrugged. "It doesn't matter. Let me tell you where the servant's chambers are. Take the third door off the kitchen and follow the hallway until you see another door. You may pick whichever room you like past that point. No one sleeps in them, so they might be a tad dank, but they are clean. Dora has a room a few doors down, and mine is the last one on the right." She nodded to me, stood and stretched—a good clue the conversation was over.

I turned and walked to the door. A thought formed.

"Ma'am, what about the roses?

"What about them?"

"Who tends to them?"

She glanced at me. "They tend to themselves."

Even the servant's quarters, folded deep into the corridors of the manor, were steeped in a mist of wild perfume. It was milder, thank God, or I would have feared suffocating in my sleep. The room I chose, the first one I entered, was designed for two people, with two narrow beds and two chairs upholstered in a salmon pink. I made a face at the room's obvious femininity. I'd never been too fond of pinks and frills and everything else I, as a young woman, was supposed to coo over.

A small desk and a single night-table with a lamp comprised the rest of the furniture. I pulled the limp pillows off one of the beds, fluffing and beating the neglect out in a sandy sprinkle. I untucked the bedcover, a deflated, sad thing, and the bedsheets, sticky with disuse.

A nagging unease followed my thoughts as I performed actions that were second nature. The whole situation in the manor was unusual, bordering on bizarre, but there was another layer to the strangeness I was experiencing—more visceral. I realized I felt watched.

Just nerves, I told myself. *The isolation getting to me.* In a few days, I'd get used to the silence. I finished spreading out the bedcover, laying my troublesome thoughts down alongside it.

"I'm here. I'll make the most of it."

There was a knock on the door. "Come in," I said.

"I brought you some tea. I'm sure you must be frozen from the trip," Dora said, entering the room. She was not graceful—she waddled more than walked—but there was an aura of activity around her that was like a furnace, heating up the house's sluggishness.

"Thank you, Dora." I sipped at the tea. Weak, with too much milk and cooling. I held my breath and drank in large gulps. She watched me in frank curiosity. Apparently, her powers at dissembling were as weak as her tea.

"I heard you came from London?" she said.

I placed the teacup down on the desk. "Yes. From Caldwell House."

She shrugged as if I'd mentioned a place in the middle of the Chinese wilderness.

"What's it like, London?"

"Um, loud. Busy. The complete opposite of this place."

"It must be wonderful to live in the center of everything, to be surrounded by different people every day."

"It's quite pleasant."

"I've lived here my whole life."

"It's beautiful here," I said.

She jerked her head up, a shadow darkening her face. "Yes, it is."

If possible, the air in the room plunged a few degrees more, and I began to see my breath as I exhaled. I shuddered.

"The cold, though, is not pleasant. How can you stand it?"

"I'm used to it. So is Ms. Simple, and Mr. Keery stays over at the stable-house, so he doesn't complain."

"He sleeps there instead of in all these empty rooms?"

"He prefers it."

"And what about Lord Grey? He must mind the chill. My previous employers would have fainted away in feverish delirium after a single night in these temperatures."

She shrugged and evaded my question. "I can bring you extra blankets, if you want."

I sighed. She wasn't going to tell me anything important, at least not yet. "Yes, that would be wonderful, Dora."

"Well, I'd best be going back to my kitchen. I have a bit of onions and carrots to chop up. We're having stew tonight. I hope that's all right?"

"Sounds delicious. Do you need any help?" As I spoke, I picked up the empty teacup and handed it to her. She extended her right arm and her sleeve peeled back, revealing a bracelet of deep cuts or scratches. The skin was raw and bruised. My hand twitched, and I looked up at her face. She had followed my eyes and smiled as she took the cup.

"No, that's all right. I can handle it on my own. You just rest." She turned and left. Questions filled my mouth.

SEVEN

I DIDN'T WANT TO SIT AND WAIT UNTIL I WAS called for dinner, and I did not feel a shadow of sleep, so I decided to walk about a bit, try to get a sense of the manor.

The servant's quarters were, as usual, separated from the center of the house. In most cases, that was not a negative thing, since the servants did not want to catch sight of their lofty employers when they were not on service duty. In Rosewood Manor, however, there was an extra hallway separating the rest of the house from the help's territory. The kitchen was located a bit closer to the front of the main hall than was normal, but I doubted it held any charms for the house's master. Most Lords and Ladies would rather crumble to ash with thirst than fetch themselves a glass of water.

The extra hallway had no doors or ornaments of any sort; not a single painting hung on the somber walls, their faces covered in a dark, gold fabric. I did not linger there and soon, I was out of our section of the house and into the main hall. I stared at the darkest set of stairs I'd ever seen, the wood the color of old blood stains, shining with such brightness I could not fathom how anyone could have scrubbed it so well.

Two other large rooms had entrances from the main hall: the dining room and the sitting room. I moved to the latter and peeked in. When I saw it was empty, I entered. There were white sheets on every piece of furniture, including, from its brougham-like girth, a piano. The sheets themselves had a thick coat of the same sticky dust I'd found everywhere, and I brushed my hand against my dress to remove it from my curious hands. How long had it been since the sitting room had been used? Months, at least.

I lifted the corner of a clammy sheet. The sofa underneath was dark, with arabesques of diluted yellow pirouetting through the fabric. Not ugly. And not nearly as blatantly extravagant as the furniture in Caldwell House. Maybe I could start in that room the following day, try to bring it back to life. Just getting rid of the white sheets would be a huge step in the right direction.

I left the sitting room and crossed to the dining room. There, at least, were signs of human influence. The long table was clean and polished, as were the chairs, and the mantelpiece poised over the large fireplace. But the room was not pretty. It had the same type of benches I'd seen as I walked into the manor, and the table was strange, its legs bent at all kinds of angles, as if getting ready to smash through the doors at any moment.

I turned and saw a gigantic mirror on the opposite side of the table, facing where the master of the house would sit each evening. The mirror was a curious one. It had no real frame, no carved wood or golden border; it lay naked, all edges plainly uncovered. I stepped up to it. Close up, it looked like any other mirror I'd ever seen.

"No accounting for taste," I muttered.

I left the strange dining room and was heading back to the kitchen when I heard a muffled crash. The noise came from the second story.

Instinctively, my feet headed toward the sound. I felt like I should do something; maybe Lord Grey was injured and in need of assistance. I crossed the room, walking toward the glimmer of the stairs.

"Where are you going, Anne?" Ms. Simple's voice echoed through the room.

I turned to face her. "I thought I heard something. A crash, from upstairs."

Her eyes flickered up the staircase, and I saw her chest move in time with her quickening breath. There was something about her reaction I did not like.

"Shouldn't we go check what happened?" I asked.

Ms. Simple cleared her throat and her gaze slipped to the floor for a few seconds. "No, it's all right. I'm sure it was nothing."

"But it was so loud."

"It's an old house, things fall and break on a daily basis. I'll see to it later."

"I could easily—"

"Come, Anne, Dora changed her mind. It seems the onions are besting her today. She's close to shriveling up after chopping just three of them."

I turned to look at the stairs again, up to where the noise had come from. Ms. Simple was probably right—just an old house stretching and dropping things.

"Yes, of course, I'll help her."

"There's a good girl."

She waited until I passed in front of her, then, stepping behind me, led me to the kitchen.

Dinner that night was an awkward affair. It was the four of us: Dora, Ms. Simple, Mr. Keery, and myself. We sat down at the kitchen table and began our meal with a prayer.

I was shocked by the leisure of the entire thing—no one rushed to pour out the stew, and no one slurped it down in anticipation of being called back to work. I was the first one finished, since I was unable to halt the habit of mindless determination toward one goal: get nourished quickly. Ms. Simple watched as I spooned undercooked vegetables into my mouth while she sipped at her broth. She smiled.

"No need to choke yourself. There's no hurry."

I looked at my companions, at their bowls, which were all more than half-full, and then at my own, which was a spoonful away from empty. I felt myself blush.

"I'm sorry. I'm so accustomed to having to hurry during mealtimes."

Ms. Simple nodded. "Yes, well, you won't be disturbed here. Eat at your own pace. We all do."

I opened my mouth, then closed it, thinking of how to word my next question.

"Ms. Simple, I'm sorry, but I did not see you set the dining room for Lord Grey's dinner. I wanted to watch you so that I would know how he prefers it."

As Ms. Simple reached for a slice of bread, her gown's collar pulled away from her throat and revealed a necklace of colors on her skin, deep purples and sickly yellows. Bruises. I frowned. They looked just like Dora's.

Ms. Simple's voice yanked my eyes back to her face. "Lord Grey eats erratically, which means whenever it pleases him, if at all. He does not encourage our disturbing him for such trivial matters as meals." She kept her eyes on the spoon in front of her.

"So, he calls to you when he is ready to dine?"

Ms. Simple shook her head. "No, we leave a covered plate on the dining table for him. He may come down whenever it's best for him."

This was most unusual. The master of a manor, a Lord, tending to his own meals? I peered at Mr. Keery, but he was concentrating on the stew before him, his face enveloped in a spider web of steam.

As soon as we were all done, I offered to help wash dishes in the hope of learning a bit more about our enigmatic employer.

I plunged my hands into the layer of soap that floated on the water, and grasped the disintegrating sponge. I began washing the bowls. Dora was quiet beside me, but I could feel her eyes turning to me every few seconds, just waiting for me to speak. I took the bait.

"What is Lord Grey like?" I asked. "He sounds so . . . different from regular Lords."

"Well, I wouldn't know. I've only had him and his father as employers, so I don't know if they are normal or not."

"How long has he been the master?"

"Our current Lord Grey took over the manor a few years ago, I think about five, after his father drowned in the fountain. Have you seen it?"

I shook my head.

"It was horrible. His son found him, all bloated." She shuddered.

"That must have been terrible for him." In truth, I was not too fond of water, so the thought of someone loosing life in that element struck deep.

"I suppose. But if the young Lord was devastated, he did not show it. He's always been a strange one, and when his father died . . . well.

He's an only child, so all the wealth was passed down to him, and we were all afraid he'd sell the estate and leave us out of work. He is not a man of many words, but that night, he called us into the parlor and reassured us no one would be dismissed. He's not left the manor since."

"He's not left in five years?" I gasped out.

Dora scraped a bowl against a pair of knives and the sound stabbed through me. She shrugged. "He has no apparent need to leave. He spends most of his time in his private rooms."

"What does he do there all day?"

She shrugged. "I don't know. We are not allowed to enter, not even to tidy up. No one has seen his chamber in years."

"That's ridiculous!"

"Not really. He brings out his bed linens when they need a good washing, as well as his chamber pot."

"I've never heard of such a thing!"

Dora laughed, a gurgling sound. "It is unusual. Not even his father did that."

"What else do you know about him?" I asked.

"He is a secretive man, always has been. I used to see a lot of him in the past, mostly when Miss Bellingham came around to the manor, but I haven't seen him much in recent years."

"Miss Bellingham? Who was she?"

"Lily Bellingham. I don't know much about her. I hadn't been moved up from floor scrubber at that time, so I had little contact with guests. I did see her once, though. She was the most beautiful woman I'd ever laid eyes on, and from the frequency of her visits, I gathered the master thought the same."

"Oh, I see."

I turned to Dora and caught a sideways glance I could make nothing of. There was an expectation on her face, like someone dipping a toe to test bathwater.

I frowned. "But, Dora, why did the rest of the household leave? If he's so wealthy, then surely he could afford to maintain them all."

She was silent for a heartbeat. Then, she put the towel down. "I have to go throw some of these ashes outside. Can you finish here?"

I nodded. Damn it. I gathered my thoughts together and finished washing and drying. I lingered a bit afterward, trailing about the different rooms, but as I saw no one else, I decided to turn in for the day.

I crossed the main hall and headed toward the servant quarters. I had a hold of my doorknob when a cold gust slithered between my feet. The coil rose up my body until every hair on my head seemed to crackle and coat over with ice. In a minute, my whole body was trembling.

What's wrong with me?

I shook my head in angry jerks, forcing the nonsense out, and entered my room, which was, thank God Almighty, many degrees warmer. Soon, I was in bed and edging toward a traveler's tired sleep, heady and hot-lidded.

EIGHT

WHATEVER INTERNAL DEVICE I POSSESSED THAT had been trained to rouse me at the same hour each morning was not fooled by my change of scenery. I woke, as usual, at half past five to a room crystallized by cold. I could not hear anyone up yet, and I considered remaining in my cocoon of blankets a bit more.

I sighed and turned over, but my body was already alert. Fine. I ripped the covers off and stood in my nightdress that still retained wisps of body heat. I threw my cloak over my shoulders and, in a very unlady-like manner, began to run and jump in place, warming my limbs up like molding clay.

Panting, I dressed in my simplest dress—opaque, dark blue with a number of wide pockets. I had no cap, and I couldn't very well wear my bonnet the whole day unless I enjoyed slamming into walls, so I wrapped my hair into a tight bun and set off for the kitchen.

I moved past Dora's room, but saw no light outlining her door— no movement at all, in fact—which, of course, meant there would be nothing hot to drink in the kitchen. I shrugged and continued. Perhaps I would find dregs of juice or a slice of bread to chew on while I waited. I lit one dim lamp in the kitchen and looked in the pantry. I found a loaf of bread, not the newest nor the most charming I'd ever seen, but a hungry stomach is not prejudiced. I cut a slice and ate it standing up, my hand cupped under my mouth to catch crumbs.

My next quest was for cleaning supplies—the usual arsenal of brooms, dusters, cloths, rags, soap, and vinegar to dilute over the floors. I found the cloths and ragged flannel squares, as well as the vinegar and the broom, but there was not a single duster in sight. Not knowing the manor well enough, I didn't want to go about opening doors. I would have to wait for Ms. Simple to point me the right way.

In ordinary circumstances, I would have needed to be given instructions for the day, a list of chores that I had to follow, but since this manor was not even in the same vicinity as "regular circumstances," I did not think anyone would mind if I took matters into my own capable hands. As I'd planned the day before, I headed to the sitting room to begin.

The winter dawn was just tapping on the windows, giving the room an eerier look than on the previous afternoon. The white sheets seemed to glow, to have life. I frowned and yanked the first sheet off. The urge to sneeze gripped my throat, and I pinched my nose to wait for it to pass.

The revealed armchair was quite beautiful, a matching set to the dark pieces I'd seen the day before. I traced the pale, yellow designs on the cushion; most likely gold thread.

I moved through the room, snatching every sheet off until they were all piled up in one corner, a great mound of cotton snow. Much better. The wooden chair and sofa limbs were dull with age, but if I'd had my proper supplies, I would have scrubbed them back to what I knew would be sparkling life. Unfortunately, the most I could settle for was to wipe them with a moist cloth.

I started with the largest piece, the sofa, and worked clockwise around the room. I allowed my hands to take over, to explore and get acquainted with the grain of the wood, the curve of the legs, the delicate carvings that required steady hands and careful care. And, as always happened while I cleaned, my thoughts stilled and quieted.

Minutes passed in absolute silence, internal and external, before my right hand came across an anomaly on one of the armchairs. I found my fingers hesitating over a corner of the wooden panel. Four deep gashes carved into the chair in almost perfect slices, done with only the sharpest of objects. For some reason, I did not want to touch them again, nor even look at them if I could avoid it.

This is silly, Anne, I told myself. *You're going to have to touch this chair for many years to come, so better get used to it.*

Perhaps, but I didn't have to do it right that minute. I moved back and turned to the last bit of furniture—a side table. As I shifted my head, I heard a soft chuckle, hoarse and deep. I stood still and held my breath, but I could not hear anything else. My heart was pounding all along my ribcage as I turned around to face whoever was in the room.

There was no one.

The sound had been so close to my ears, it would have been impossible for the person to move out of the room with such speed without a sound.

I stepped into the hallway, but there was nothing different; the rising sun still poured through an empty corridor. I frowned.

"Now you're hallucinating. Wonderful." I shook my head. It must have been my imagination.

Just in case, I grabbed the broom and cloths and moved to the dining room. There'd be plenty of time for the sitting room when the rest of the household woke. There was nothing to fear, I knew that. But I wasn't dumb, either.

Soon enough, the meager household rose. I was halfway through scrubbing the dining room table when I heard Dora laughing, an echo that reached me all the way from the kitchen. The laughter soon unwound itself and became a few choice curse words, followed by the sharp smell of burnt bread. I hesitated. I could go assist Dora, but I feared she'd be insulted at my sailing in, efficiency personified, to rescue her from her mediocre skills.

But I also did not want to eat burnt bread.

I wiped my hands and went to the kitchen. There were smoke circles around Dora's head while she attempted to salvage some of the bread slices from a sure death.

"Dora, stop. You'll burn yourself," I said.

She turned. A soot smudge trailed down her already sweating face. "I hate throwing food away. It's just a disgrace! I can't even manage toast!"

I moved her aside, grabbing the large fork that punctured the piece of bread over the fire. The particular slice in question looked like fireplace scraps. Probably tasted like it, too.

"Look, I'll show you. There's nothing to it once you see it."

I cut some new slices, making sure they were thick enough so that the large fork would not tear through the bread, and placed one over the fire. A few seconds of flame, then flip over, that was it. I then put the slice on a plate and added a dollop of creamy butter.

"Do you have some brown sugar and some cinnamon?" I asked Dora.

Her eyes watched my hands. "I think so. Why?"

"Let me show you my trick." I stretched a hand as she went into the pantry for the required items. She returned with two glass bottles, both full of auburn specks. I took a pinch of each and sprinkled them on every plate, letting the sugar and cinnamon rest on the butter that clung to the bread.

"That's it. Mary, Caldwell House's cook, taught me that. It makes all the difference, you'll see."

"Thanks." Dora's smile was tight, her face a tad flushed. Damn it, I should have let her serve the sooty slices. I fetched Ms. Simple, who was already on her way, followed by the even paler Mr. Keery.

We sat down to tea and toast, once again around the battle-wounded kitchen table.

"Dora, this is outstanding," Ms. Simple said. She raised the corner of her bread to her eyes. "Is this cinnamon?"

Dora nodded.

"Well, you've outdone yourself. Wonderful."

I kept my eyes on my plate and let Dora scoop up all the praise. No need to start making enemies so early in the day.

"Ms. Simple, I was wondering where you keep the dusters and floor wax? I tried to find them this morning, but I'm afraid I had no luck."

"Yes, I saw you'd begun already. Removed the sheets off the sitting room furniture. That was not necessary."

I stopped chewing. Bloody hell. "I thought I'd give the furniture a good scrub."

"That's all well and good, but the sheets must return to their proper places."

"But—"

"I'm sorry, Anne, but the master hates to see the sofas and such uncovered in the sitting room, so right after you've finished your meal, please begin replacing them."

"Couldn't I at least swap those sheets for new ones? They are dragging dust," I said, while my fingernails dug into the table's wood. Now I saw how the marks on its surface had been made.

"That's up to you. If you really find the old sheets that repulsive, then, by all means, replace them. The master must not to come down and see everything uncovered, so please, I want it all back to normal within the hour. That should be enough time, don't you think?"

"Yes, ma'am."

"There's no need for 'ma'am.' Just call me Ms. Simple."

I nodded and finished my tea in silence. I chanced a look at Dora, who had a bright smile on her peach lips. Next time, I'd let her burn the house down before lifting a single utensil to help her.

NINE

THROUGHOUT THE AFTERNOON, I LISTENED FOR a repetition of the morning's noise, but caught nothing of interest. The house was still, as if balancing over a precipice, afraid any loud word would send it crashing down to the waters below. Not too pleasant, but I supposed I'd get used to it soon enough.

I finished washing floors and began the arduous task of polishing silver. There wasn't much of it, considering the size of the manor, or at least, not much that I could see. Lord Grey could have had it all stashed away in his chambers, the silver turning dull in seclusion. My fingers turned into cramped lumps, covered in the viscous goo that I swabbed onto the platters, tea sets and dinnerware.

No one disturbed me. I wondered what Ms. Simple and Dora were up to in the drowsy afternoon. In all honesty, with a household as diminished as Rosewood's, I could not understand why a housekeeper was needed at all, but I was not about to question the way things were run. I'd already fumbled with Dora. And on top of it all, I missed Elsie. Waves of homesickness swept over me as all the little tasks reminded me of her, of her silliness and her willingness to laugh no matter the hour or the circumstance. Laughter seemed to be in short order in Rosewood.

When I finished with the blasted silver, I found I did not know what else to occupy my time with, so I went in search of Ms. Simple to see if anything still required my attention. I found her in her room, reading.

"If you are finished with your tasks, you are free to do as you like until supper. May I ask that you return to the kitchen a bit earlier to check on Dora? I'm not foolish enough to think she developed culinary skills at the precise moment we have another member in our home. If you could show her whatever tips you can, all our digestive systems would appreciate it." She gave me a queasy smile.

"Yes, Ms. Simple." I would be doing nothing of the sort.

I trailed out to the front hall, passing the once again sheet-smothered sitting room. Having nothing to do was an uncomfortable state. My hands itched to be put to work and, for one surreal moment, I even considered doing some sewing. Thank God another idea came to my rescue. What if I took a walk around the grounds? I listened for any reasons why I shouldn't and heard none. So I returned to my room to fetch my cloak and then entered the winter afternoon.

The roses looked the same as the day before, and I wondered, neither for the first nor the last time, how they could bloom with such fervent enthusiasm in the hostile climate. The snow was a soft powder under my feet as I made a turn around the house to where I'd seen Mr. Keery take the horses. A wooden building stretched before me, closed off to my eyes, but not to my nose. I could smell the rich, chocolate scent of horses, the wild hint of hay, the warm, leather saddles. I inhaled and smiled.

Farther down was a copse of trees, their figures crowded around a spot in the middle of them. The closer I got, the more uneasy I became, my ears twitching with the crackle of tension I could feel. I was about to turn back when I caught a sliver of glittering water through the thick trees.

Water was not a close friend of mine, but I moved toward it, pulled by its gurgle. There, in the center, was a large fountain. I frowned. Why would anyone put a fountain so far from the house, where it couldn't be seen?

It was rather plain, with only one cascade of reluctant liquid, but there was something about it that sent my knees knocking together. It was made of black marble, with no pebbles of inconsistency, no lines, no cracks. The water reflected the trees around it so that the effect was a cameo, silhouettes of trees against the black background. I had just raised a hand to touch the edge when the distracting sensation of being watched returned. I shifted, making a loose circle around me, but saw no one. So much for a relaxing stroll. I turned to leave, but a piece of my cloak caught on a nearby branch. I tugged at it. It would not come loose, so I had to maneuver around to grip the branch. I had not noticed how sharp some of the smaller twigs were, wooden skewers that took offense all too easily. I cried out when one of them punctured my right palm in a hot stab.

With an angry jerk, my cloak came loose. A thin trickle of blood spattered the churned snow and I cursed, bringing my palm up to my lips. I walked back to the house, sucking on my punctured hand every once in a while, until I came around the corner and headed toward the front door.

On the opposite side, next to a grouping of yet more skeletal trees, was the outline of a man. He turned in my direction and held my gaze through the dimming, bland light. I blinked, and he was gone.

"I saw someone on the grounds," I announced around the table, picking at my liquefied potatoes and charred chicken breast. Ms. Simple stopped chewing.

"Where?"

"By the side of the house. He was standing very still."

No one said anything for a few minutes.

"It was probably the master, he enjoys the occasional stroll in the afternoon," said Ms. Simple.

"Oh. I should have curtsied or something. I just stood, staring."

Dora moved her greasy fork. "He won't care. Most likely, he did not even see you."

I kept quiet, but I could still see that figure, the unseen eyes weighing me down like stones.

Three weeks passed. I wasn't getting any more used to the food, but the hours were settling down into routine, unlike the dust I was trying to scourge from the manor. I'd never seen a place in such a state.

I spent my mornings in the dining and sitting rooms, polishing and scrubbing while Dora cursed at the stove and various other kitchen devices. The smells that drifted in were ghastly, but I'd learned my lesson and kept my feet out of her culinary domain.

The routine was only broken one day a week, when the man who delivered our vegetables and meat rumbled up the long path to the manor on his cart. Ms. Simple would put on her best shawl, and Dora would run a much-needed comb through her hair, all to meet the man from the nearby town. I watched from the doorway as the three of them chatted, rare laughter filling the winter air.

There were never any letters for either woman, but they always asked and made the man, John, look through his bag. I had a suspicion they went through those motions each week to hold his attention a while longer, to brush against a life that was so removed from theirs just a few minutes more.

I enjoyed watching them during those times, when the heaviness I didn't understand lifted off them, and they prattled on like any two women in a London market.

I enjoyed those days as much as they.

On one afternoon, in which I found myself idle again, I decided to set out on a bit of a thorough exploration, long overdue. Not outside this time, but inside. Ms. Simple and Dora were in their rooms, Mr. Keery was in the stables as usual, and the master was . . . wherever he liked to spend his time, so I had little incentive to curb my curiosity.

I waited until the house was silent around me, then set out deeper into its bowels, past the staircase, past the edge of what I knew. Whatever hope had been chirping inside me about what I'd find slowly began to strangle itself with the cold that seemed to grow the farther into the manor I moved. Just a few paces past the staircase and the trembling in my hands became pretty severe. There had to be a broken windowpane somewhere. This could not be normal, even in such a large, stone-crafted house.

Plunging my hands into my pockets, I moved forward. The walls were tight around me, the wallpaper faded by a sun that no longer appeared to reach down these passages, the smell dank with neglect. No one had come down to look at, let alone clean, any of the rooms that were hidden behind the forbidding doors. I tested one, to make sure, and found it locked, the latch hitching with a metallic cough. Well, at least I wouldn't be expected to dust in there.

I tried two more doors, but by that time, my hands were shaking to such a degree that I knew I had to turn back, or risk illness. It seemed the house would keep its secrets. And I'd found one more direction in which I couldn't travel on the grounds. Wonderful.

As I was turning around to retrace my chilled steps, I thought I heard something—another chuckle. Had I disturbed the master? But as I tried to part the dim light, I could see no one. Fear joined in chorus with the cold to get my legs moving. My head screamed that I needed to get back to the main hall. I didn't know why I was so panicked, which scared me as much as the fear itself did.

Finally, I could see the hall; the sunlight that bathed its floor paused on the edge of darkness, not daring to brush through it. I passed the staircase, stepping fully into the sun. Sighing with relief, I turned and peered into the darkness that had spat me back out.

I shivered. It seemed to peer back.

Close to dinner time, and more out of boredom than actual need, I climbed the stairs to polish the landing. I hadn't been to the second story yet, and while it was as cold as the rest of the manor, it had a lovely view of the grounds. The windows had no curtains, and fully allowed a glimpse of the surrounding forest, the trees so close to one another I could hardly see the snowy earth.

Finding my hands all too soon straying from the work I'd set for myself, I gave it up altogether. Who would care to check up on me, especially since it wasn't one of my approved duties? A rather convincing argument, I found. So I gave myself up to the sight of the sun setting over the flock of trees.

It was a soothing moment, allowing me to even forget, somewhat, the strange atmosphere that prevailed in the manor, that sense of some-thing hidden and not too friendly.

The sun burnt, large against the trees. I'd never seen it quite like that before. In London, I'd always gotten just a peek of its mantle as it lowered, its beauty crushed by buildings and smoke, but here, it was magnificent. First, it burnt orange, then red, lending the landscape its warmth for a few more minutes. One of its rays caught a tendril of my hair in its light. A flash of color wrapped around me, triggering a memory I didn't even know I possessed: a woman's face, frowning as she looked at something behind me, her hair a crown of gold on her head, resplendent with sun. My mother.

Pain grabbed me. Like a hand tightening around my heart, I felt grief taking over my body. For most of my life, I'd been rather independent, as any servant with a father like mine had to be, but at that moment, watching the sun die over the barrier of trees, feeling the cold growing by the second, all I wanted was a comforting arm around my shoulders. A voice to tell me that things would be just fine.

When I felt a tear coursing down my cheek, I shook my head. What nonsense. I just missed Elsie, that was all. And my home.

No, I chided myself. Caldwell House was no longer my home. This manor, with all its faults, with all its strangeness, was where I belonged now.

"Supper, Anne!" Dora's voice screeched up the stairs.

"Coming."

Good, supper, and then bed. I'd feel better in the morning.

As I began to turn away from the window, I saw movement near the borderline of trees. I frowned and looked closer. There was that figure again. Although I was sure he had to be the master, he looked . . . peculiar. The word came into my head without any real basis in fact. He was dressed nicely enough, he moved with elegance, but still, there was something about him that I couldn't quite place.

Looking down at the figure, I thought of what Dora had told me the night I'd arrived. Why did he choose to live so isolated?

Without any warning, the man turned, raised his head, and looked directly at me.

I gasped and raced down the stairs.

Later that night, scratches at my door woke me from a restless slumber. I swam up through the layers of twisted dreams to the dark and cold of my room. My heart was pounding, and my breath insisted on abandoning my lungs with such force it burned through my throat. I lay still. For a moment, I thought I'd imagined the sound, that it had just been a dream's tail disappearing around my ears. But then, I heard it again—scratching.

I didn't know if there were any animals in the manor, but I doubted it. Except for Mr. Keery, no one else seemed the type to care for pets. Rats were never out of the question, even in such a grand house, but even that thought rang false in my head. I grit my teeth and unwound my limbs from the sheets.

"Bloody hell!" I exclaimed as the cold struck me. I could see my breath again. I looked over to the window. It was closed and bolted, something I had checked again and again before retiring to bed. There had to be a draft. How could the temperature change like that, in dips and plunges?

I walked to the door. The scratching continued, lazy and regular, like a cat grooming itself. As I neared the noise, though, it stopped.

Holding my breath, I inched an ear against the wood in the hopes of hearing either a retreating creature or maybe some panting. Anything that would solve the mystery and allow me to return to my warm, body-shaped dent on the bed. I could hear nothing, though. No breathing, no sighing, no panting.

In the time it took for me to blink, the scratches began again, fiercer and faster, like knives stabbing the wood. The sound rose higher until it reached where my ear had rested seconds before.

I considered screaming. My mouth opened, but no sound flew out. The cold clutched at my voice.

I couldn't explain what happened next, all I knew was that I felt a pulsing slightly above my ribcage, like a low drumming that rose, spreading a rhythm that chanted of warmth and strength. It poured out my panic and refilled my body with tranquility.

I lifted my hands to my eyes. My fingers felt so hot I was sure there was something wrong with them, but no, they looked just like always: a bit scuffed, but reliable. I felt dizzy, and my limbs threatened to collapse in a pile around me. So I did the only thing I could think of, I gripped the doorknob and yanked the door open.

A gust of winter air surrounded me, and I tore at it with my hands, flinging it off me like torn spider webs. The cold seemed to be sucked out of my room, and I could soon breathe again without the stabs of air against my fumbling insides.

A weakness scurried up my legs and I had to grip on to the door. I concentrated on staying upright as I pressed my hot forehead to the tranquil wood. As with the two previous times, the spell soon passed. I stepped out into the corridor, but it was empty and quiet, not a single light staining the floorboards.

My breathing was too fast, too shallow. I had to slow it down or risk fainting, which, after what I'd just heard and felt, was not the wisest idea. Clutching my shaking hands together, I concentrated on slow, even breaths. *It had just been an animal*, I told myself. As much as my mind resisted it, it was the only explanation. Unless I'd gone and truly lost my mind.

By slow degrees, I got myself back under control. As tired as I felt, I knew sleep would not return that night, so I pulled my Bible out and lit my lamp. Wrapping the blanket tightly around me, I buried myself in the pages. I waited for the comfort of my father's voice to still my thoughts and fears, but it never came.

TEN

I MENTIONED THE PREVIOUS NIGHT'S disturbance around the kitchen table the following morning. By that time, I had managed to convince myself of my own fright's silliness. I'd checked the door as soon as the sun had trailed in on dim footsteps and had seen nothing on the entirety of it. I made an effort not to allow myself to quake at a single night of lost sleep. I spoke of the incident in the lightest tone, a layer of laughter anchoring the words as I uttered them.

The room, however, stopped in its tracks. Everything and everyone around me appeared to stop breathing, hearts paused in mid-beat. The silence drew my eyes up from my coffee cup, allowing me to catch a look exchanged between Ms. Simple and Dora.

Ms. Simple cleared her throat. "What type of scratching did you hear, Anne?"

"It sounded like an animal asking to be let in. Are there any dogs or cats in the manor?"

Dora shook her head. Her hair was so resplendent, it seemed to have the sun nestling in its folds.

"There are no pets in the house," she said.

"It could have been rats," I said.

"Could be." Ms. Simple paused. "Just in case, Anne, make certain you bolt your door before you sleep."

My mouth went dry, an aftertaste of burnt coffee on my tongue. "Ms. Simple, why should I lock the door? If it was a rat, it couldn't possibly reach the doorknob, let alone turn it."

I looked over at Mr. Keery, who had remained silent throughout the entire meal. His eyes were not on me, but I could see an intricate system of red threads tangling around his eyeballs.

"Mr. Keery, what do you think? Could it have been rats?" I asked.

He flicked his gaze over me. "I don't know, miss. It's possible." His voice cracked.

I didn't believe any of them. They knew something. What was happening at Rosewood Manor?

I noticed the cold wasn't as sharp as the previous days as I scrubbed the main hall later that morning. For the first time, I found I was sweating in thick drops that dove to stain the floors I'd just cleaned.

The hall, when I got down to polishing it, was much larger than it appeared and much more intricate in its designs than I'd noticed. It was ornate in a veiled manner, the carvings and detailing unlike Caldwell House's chilling bad taste. The stone floors themselves were a work of careful art, with tight symbols on the edges of each separate tile. When I'd seen them that first day, I had assumed the markings were just a vain frame on the stones, but as I scrubbed, the shapes became distinct. No two were the same in a single tile. I ran a finger over the shallow designs, and I could have sworn some of them shifted under my touch.

I was still kneeling on the floor when I heard footsteps behind me on the stairs. A gust of scented air followed the sound—the black smell of snuffed candles and the ever-present rose perfume. I felt a pause, both in myself and in the person behind me. I removed my hands from the stones with a tug (they did not want to part with the etchings), and brushed them against my dress as I stood to greet the person I was sure was Rosewood's master.

I turned and lifted my eyes to the stairs. There was no one there. Just the smoky scent tumbling through the air.

I didn't bring that encounter up with any of them during our midday meal. There seemed little point in sharing when they kept their own thoughts tight between the three of them. Although, I was beginning to doubt Mr. Keery's involvement. Each time I saw him, he was reduced, like a photograph left in the sun, growing lighter and lighter until it sank into the white background. I feared one morning he would disappear before my eyes, leaving a half-empty plate abandoned on the table.

The cold returned in the afternoon, fighting with the sun for dominance over the floor and walls. My sweat dried in sections on my body, so that, at any one moment, chills ran up and down different patches of my skin.

I finished my scant duties with less care than was my usual, but I had to get out of the manor. One more second in that grey prison and I'd collapse in a heap, waiting for my blood to congeal.

The sun was a relief. I moved in the opposite direction I'd taken the day before and toward where I'd seen the figure, but I soon had to stop. The trees were woven with such tightness, I feared to attempt an entrance. Besides, there was no sun in that direction and gust after gust of pine breath pushed me back.

Fine. I walked back around to the stables and soon reached the large, black fountain. I didn't want to be there. It seemed sinister amid all the whiteness. I tried to step back and yet realized I was moving forward, toward the curved rim. The afternoon's silence hardened against me, choking off my crunching footsteps.

Hesitating, I placed a hand on the surface. It was cold enough to burn fingers off. How was it possible the water still flowed? It should have turned into a disk of ice long ago.

I peered over the edge, gripping the stone with two claw-like hands. My face floated amid the blackness, my eyes almonds of water staring straight at me. As I drew back, there was a ripple and the flash of a face. It was vague, but before my eyes blurred with water and salty fear, I saw two circles, deep and red, looking down at me from around my shoulder.

A cascade of bird screams soaked the air.

I didn't have time to do anything but gasp. A hand, as burning as the stone fountain, clutched my neck and pushed me down into the black water. The liquid forced itself into my ears, pried open my lips in a scream that hovered, unheard. My hands pushed against the floor, but I could not budge. I clawed at the grip that held me, but it evaded me. There was nothing pushing me down, and yet, I could not rise. My vision rippled and fogged over, an edge of dark lace tightening around me.

Then I felt two very real hands suck me back up out of the water, into the loud air bristling with shrieking birds. There was an uncomfortable heat where the hands had been, and my hair was limp and soggy against my eyes. As I took a gasping breath, the air came into my lungs with the sting of alcohol. I collapsed to the ground, coughing, while a set of voices—one high and resonant like sun glinting off a key, the other low and throaty— spoke above me. I could not understand the words, and in any case, I would not have cared to hear what they were saying.

With one last low chuckle, the dark voice stopped, and with it, the angry bird calls.

I coughed until my sides knotted up, ignoring everything around me except the wheezing that ripped in and out of my chest. Footsteps padded on the snow, stepping close to my kneeling form. A breeze brushed me as the figure lowered itself down to a crouch. I took some deep breaths, slow and steady, trying to keep the coughing down, and when the spasms released me, I lifted my ashen face.

There, kneeling before me was the master of Rosewood Manor.

ELEVEN

"IT WAS FOOLISH OF YOU TO TOUCH THE fountain." His voice was a shadow of what I'd just heard, its light muted. I tried to focus on him to stop the horror I'd felt in the last few moments from overwhelming me. As I began to shiver uncontrollably, my panicked eyes landed on the ones in front of me.

He was not what I'd expected, although, I wasn't even sure what I had thought he'd look like. Not so thin, for one thing. He looked like a collection of bones that had agreed to join in locomotion. His cheekbones seemed to rub against his skin. A shiny wave of brown hair wrapped around his head, the lanky locks beaded in dew drops of sweat despite the cold.

And then his eyes—I'd never seen anything like them. A speckled marble of golds and greens, a mantle of shifting colors. His face looked like something out of a painting, crafted with skill and strange, cold beauty. There was an intelligence to it that belied his youth. He could almost have looked kind, but his eyes gave him away. Too sharp.

"Make sure you do not come this way again." He threw me another look and shifted his meager weight to stand.

"Sir, thank you. I don't know what happened, but I'd surely be dead if it weren't for your presence." Speaking was an effort, every consonant threatening to send me coughing.

"Yes, you would be dead. Let that be a lesson."

I stood, my hands almost grasping the fountain once again, but a look from Lord Grey and I flung them back. He made no attempt to help me stand.

"But sir, what happened? Who—"

He didn't allow me to finish. "You are the new maid," he said.

I took a deep breath. "Yes, sir. Anne Tinning, from Caldwell House."

I could see his hands, emaciated and bruised, trembling against his sides. In an instant, one of them flew up to his face to cover a cough—a racking, dry sound that hurt me just from listening to it. He shouldn't have been outside in the cold. Not that the manor's interior was much better.

"Sir, are you quite all right?"

"Of course I am." His voice was no louder than a murmur, yet lined with knife blades. His whole body seemed to sway, and I feared he would crumple to the snow before me.

"Anne, is it?"

I nodded. "Yes, sir."

"Fine. Now, go inside." He moved his head in the manor's direction. "I'm sure there are things to be dusted or scrubbed or whatever it is you maids do."

I tried not to rear back at his words. "Yes, sir." I curtsied.

His eyes widened, and he began to gasp in quiet laughter. I could do nothing but stand there until he finished.

"Very amusing. Now, go inside."

Wrapping my cloak around my still shivering body, I passed by Lord Grey. I could feel his eyes inhaling my every move, and I shivered.

"Tell Ms. Simple to give you something strong. Otherwise, I'll have one less maid, and as I'm sure you've noticed, I can ill afford it."

"Yes, sir."

He gave a dry chuckle.

I did not turn around, but kept my feet on the path to the front door. I could hear no steps behind me. I looked, just once, before I opened the door, but did not see Lord Grey.

Ms. Simple was crossing the main hall as I entered, and her eyes stretched as she took in my seaweed hair, my paleness, my shaking.

"Whatever happened to you, Anne?" she asked.

What could I say? No one would tell me the truth, anyway. When I spoke, my voice was quivering more than I'd have preferred. "I had an accident. Lord Grey assisted me."

Ms. Simple's lips tightened. "Yes, well, come on, child. Let's get something to warm you up."

No one, not even I, spoke of what had happened to me. There was a forced lightness to our supper, the conversation ringing with laughter that petered out as soon as it left our tight mouths. Dora kept eyeing me as if I were about to disintegrate before her very eyes, while Ms. Simple served me slice after slice of tasteless beef roast. My hands continued to shake with the shock, but I gripped my utensils tighter and did my best to pretend the last couple of hours hadn't occurred.

As soon as I could manage it, I excused myself and left their company.

It was still too early to retire for the day, but I needed a bit of solitude to examine what had happened at the black fountain's foot.

I went from room to room, my eyes checking for traces of dust or dirt as my thoughts churned through my head. I was sure of what I'd experienced. I could still feel the weight that had forced itself on my body, the imprint of hands burned into my scalp and neck. I rubbed the sore spots as I entered the dining room.

I caught sight of the mirror. Perhaps there were actual marks on my skin, evidence I could turn to when belief sagged. The room was dressed in shadows, since no one had bothered to light lamps or even candles. The curtains were not drawn, however, so thin hairs of moonlight dangled in the air. I felt them brush me with softness as I reached the strange mirror. I gazed in and gasped.

The moonlight had revealed what the sun had not, a layer of symbols swimming under the glass's surface. The same type of writing I'd seen on the stone tiles in the main hall. But how was it possible? They were etched under the glass, or maybe into the thin skin of mirror itself. I lifted a hand, all thoughts of the marks on my body forgotten, and almost brushed the smooth surface.

"It appears we have not learnt our lesson today."

Through the mirror, I could see Lord Grey's figure half melted in shadow. I turned around and clasped my hands behind me.

"I'm sorry, sir." I looked down at the floor, thankful the moon could not reveal my burning cheeks. There was a long moment of silence.

"Is the floor very interesting, Anne?"

I flinched. "No, sir." I lifted my gaze, heavy and hot.

Lord Grey walked to the table, where his plate was lying, covered and waiting.

"If you don't mind, Anne, I'm going to have dinner. Or is it lunch? I can't remember when I last ate." His voice was like the sea at night, the waves coming in and out of darkness. Some words were brushed by light, some cool with black.

"Of course, sir. I'll go." I curtsied before remembering how he'd taken my last clumsy attempt. He did not laugh this time.

"That's not what I meant. If you don't have pressing engagements, I'd like a few words with you."

Hmm. Only a few days and I'd already earned a reprimand. "Of course, sir."

"Will you please take a seat?" He motioned to the table. I blinked.

"Sir, do you mean, in a chair?"

"No, I mean in mid-air. In a chair, Anne."

Lord Grey pulled back his seat at the head of the grotesque table and sat without a sound.

"Would you like me to light a candle or lamp, sir?"

"No, that's quite all right."

My hands shook as I grasped the chair I'd scrubbed that morning and every morning for the past three weeks, sitting down on the tip of the seat, allowing only the minimum of my body contact with the grand furniture.

"Would you like some wine?" he asked as he uncovered the decanter before him.

"No, sir, thank you."

"I suppose it's just as well. I don't know where Dora keeps the bloody glasses."

My head jerked up at the tone, but he was already sipping at the thick liquid. He began cutting his meat. His hands were steady now, no trace of the twitching I'd seen earlier, but they had cuts on them, puckered edges of skin drying with blood. I winced as he brought a piece of meat up to his lips, knowing the horror of Dora's cooking, but he made no sign. He ate with an air of distraction, as if his mind were pacing far away while his body nourished itself.

After a few bites, he set his instruments down on the plate and lowered his hands to his lap.

"You must take care not to go about touching things in this house," he said. "Certain things do not take kindly to being disturbed." His forehead creased and his eyes shifted to look past me, toward the mirror.

"Yes, sir. I understand." But I did not understand. Objects that complained of being touched?

"Not that mirror, though. You could have touched that without consequence. Or, at least, nothing more than a smudge, as I'm sure you know, being the expert in all that."

He blinked and pulled his eyes back to me. "It is a strange glass, isn't it?

"Yes, sir. Very beautiful."

"Beautiful? I'd never thought of it that way." He laughed, allowing the moonlight to brush his voice. A second later, the sound twisted as his voice hitched into a cough. He took a deep breath. "It is of my own design."

That gave me pause. If he'd designed it, how could he not have thought it beautiful?

With a suddenness that surprised me, he rose from his chair and crossed the room, his thin frame all angles in the gloom. He stepped right before the mirror.

"Hmm. You're right, Anne. It is quite pretty." He passed a hand over its surface. "Look."

What did he want now? I cursed myself for walking into the dining room in the first place. I inched close to Lord Grey, who still had his hand on the glass.

"Put your hand here."

Oh, for the love of everything good and holy. I walked over and joined him in front of the mirror. My left hand hovered over its surface for an instant, until I finally pressed it into place with a sigh. As soon as my skin brushed the cold surface, a jolt slithered through my fingers, pushing my hand back, off the mirror. I gasped and yanked my hand as far away from the glass as I could get. What in God's name?

"Sir, what—"

Lord Grey's expression stopped my voice. His eyes narrowed as he stepped away from me. He looked at my palm, his face as cold as the stones beneath us.

"Interesting," he said. He looked at the mirror once more, then walked out of the room without another word.

I glanced down at my palm. The symbols I'd touched were on the surface, their strange angles stitched into my skin.

TWELVE

THAT NIGHT, WHEN THE SCRATCHES BEGAN again, I felt more anger than fear as I ripped the covers off and stood. Sleep dragged at me, making me feel heavy and thick. All I wanted was to get some rest. Whatever blasted animal was amusing itself by waking decent people at indecent hours had better hope it could run, because if I caught it . . .

But when I opened the door, the entire corridor was empty. A low laugh brushed by me—a wind of cold tagging me, then moving down the hallway. I covered my eyes with my hands and shook my head. What was going on? The paralyzing cold had returned, making me quiver with spasms of protesting muscles.

As I lowered my hands, a glow appeared, hovering on my right, where our corridor fused with the extra, empty hallway. I did not even stop to grab a shawl before I set my bare feet to trace after it. I ran.

The light, a candle from the look of it, moved forward, toward the main hall. I chased it, inhaling the dark smell of wax, but I could not see who was holding the flame. At last, it seemed to pause by the foot of the stairs.

I wished I hadn't drawn the curtains, since the moonlight would have unveiled the person in front of me, but the shadows seemed to feed off the candle, crowding around it in hunger. With a sweep, the light rose up the stairs, one step at a time. Why I began to follow is a mystery, but I was powerless to do otherwise. The hand I'd placed on the mirror began to itch with a force I'd never experienced before, making me want to peel back my skin and scratch it from the inside.

I grasped the banister (it was too dark, and I was too tired to worry about my fingerprints) and placed a foot on the smooth surface of the stairs. The glow bobbed like a cork, seeming to grow brighter the more steps I climbed. My eyes felt huge, full of warm light, and all I wanted was to rest them, just for a second.

I must have closed them, because the stab of pain that shot up from my newly tattooed palm forced my eyes open. And just in time to see a shadow rush at me, striking me with its full force. It felt as if a sack of ice had been thrown against me. If I hadn't been fully conscious and gripping the banister, I would have been thrown down those massive stairs. Probably killed.

As it was, it took all my strength to defy gravity. A shriek tore through the air, rushing past my ears and down the long corridor. My heart would not quiet down; I held my hand over my mouth to keep from screaming.

I began to hear sounds from the servant's quarters. Doors opening, voices muffled by the walls. I could pick out Dora's voice. My legs threatened to give out under me, but I ignored them as I sidestepped down the staircase.

Once I reached the steady floor, I launched into a sprint through the main hall, down the deserted corridor and into our space.

Dora and Ms. Simple turned at my steps. They were both blue with cold, their hands clasped inside their sleeves to keep them from shaking. Ms. Simple was standing before my door, which was ripped off its hinges, the wood looking limp and bruised. The housekeeper extended one hand and pointed inside.

On the floor, torn to countless shreds, was my Bible.

I must admit, the assault shook me. That Bible had been the only item I had from my father, my only tie to my real family, and now, it lay scattered throughout the room, some pieces looking as if they'd actually been chewed and spat out. Anger replaced fear and took a firm hold of me. I would find out who'd done something so unforgivable. The secrets had gone on long enough.

I never did get back to bed, not that I could have slept even if I had. Mr. Keery managed to put my door back in place, but it looked rather damaged. I considered switching rooms.

As I peeled piece after piece of the sacred words off my floor (some so translucent that the words seemed written on the wooden boards themselves), Ms. Simple stepped into my room.

She appeared to have gathered herself together, smoothing out her bewilderment.

"The master would like to see you," she said from the doorway.

I stood. "Of course. Where is he waiting?"

"In his private chambers."

"Should I go alone, Ms. Simple?" I had never been in such a position before, having to report to my male employer without at least having his manservant in the same room. My stomach knotted.

"He has asked that you come alone. He won't harm you." She smiled gently and looked me over. "But make yourself decent first, child."

I realized I was still in my stiff nightdress, the cold now a permanent part of the fabric, and barefoot. Ms. Simple closed the door and I dressed with speed, not bothering to do much more to my hair than submit it to a rough brushing. If Lord Grey could not bother to care about my reputation, I would not bother to pin my hair up.

Of course, once I made it up the stairs, with no small effort on my body's part (it bucked at putting itself in danger again), I realized I had no clue which were the master's chambers. There were at least ten different doors near me, and I could see many corners that could each have revealed ten more, for all I knew.

I was about to knock on the first door, ready to try them all, when I heard that soft voice, flooded with light, coming from a room at the end of the passage.

"Anne, my rooms are here."

I followed the sound, more than a little annoyed at the familiar tone. Yes, he had saved my life, but did he now think I belonged to him?

When I reached the room, Lord Grey was holding the door open an inch, his eyes peeking at me in curiosity.

"Come in." He allowed the door to swing away. I took a single step inside as he moved to a seat nearby.

There was an ocean of early sunlight touching every surface in the room, making countless jars and containers ripple. Some were empty, while others were stuffed with leaves and crackling seeds. The smell was cloying—sweet red cinnamon, acrid lemon peels, snapping ginger roots. All blended and stewing together, the roses' scent hovering over the entirety of it. The antechamber should have been huge, but it was so crammed with books—leaning or standing on each other—and containers that it appeared much smaller.

"Is it to your liking?" His words yanked me back, my face growing warm as I realized I'd been staring at everything around me. His eyes never left my face, and I raised my own gaze, bit by bit, until it was level with his.

In the morning light, Lord Grey seemed young—much younger than I'd first estimated. He was only a few years older than I. His features were sharp; his mouth, a still horizon. A handsome, if troubled, face. But the thinness was impossible to veil, even in the robe he wore. I could see his bones sticking up against the cloth. With that cough he had, he could not be well.

"Would you care to sit?" He pointed to a chair piled with books. "I could move them."

"No, sir, it's quite all right."

His lip curled. "Not one for sitting, are you, Anne?"

I squeezed out a smile.

"Never mind. I heard about what happened during the night, the business with the Bible and all that. Most unfortunate."

"Yes, sir."

"I trust you were not injured?"

"No, sir."

"Is there anything you'd like to ask me?"

What the bloody hell did he want me to say? "No, sir."

"I'm sure being almost drowned, attacked on the stairs, and finding your book torn to shreds would pose some questions."

I felt a pressure against me, almost as if someone were resting a cloak on me—one made from threads of ice. Lord Grey rose and walked toward me. The pressure slinked off.

"Well?"

"Sir, how did you know I was attacked on the stairs? I did not share that with anyone."

He ignored my words, turning from me and toward one of the windows. "Anne, are you religious?"

I pressed a hand to my forehead. The riddles were getting to be a nuisance.

"No, sir."

"What about the Bible?"

"It was a gift from my father, sir."

"Are you baptized?"

"Yes, sir. My father insisted."

"But you are not a practicing Christian or Catholic."

"Practicing? No, sir. I've attended services for years while in Lady Caldwell's service, but I would not call myself a devout attendee."

He could have sacked me for that, but since I'd seen no evidence the household ever attended church, I risked it.

"Good. That will be all for now, Anne. Return after lunch. I rather think these rooms are in need of some dusting."

"Of course, sir." I curtsied to his back and stepped out of the room. Was everyone in the manor out of their minds?

THIRTEEN

WHEN I RETURNED TO LORD GREY'S ROOMS IN the early afternoon (after much sighing from Ms. Simple and glinting sidelong glances from Dora), the door was wide open and the master was dressed. All in black, he looked like a languishing crow.

"You can begin there." He pointed to a corner that had been swallowed by a pile of books. Gravity seemed non-existent as small tomes suspended gigantic ones on their quaking covers. My hands hovered over them.

"Sir, excuse me, but where can I move these books to?"

"Here, hand them to me. I'll find homes for them." He came to stand behind me, his frame casting a thin, long shadow on the wall.

Lifting the first dark book, I saw the cover simmering with strange symbols. I handed it to Lord Grey, who moved about the room on silent feet, a ripple of energy as he peeked into stuffed bookcases and gasping side tables, only pausing when a coughing spell overtook him. One by one, he found new places for the entire tower of books.

I began dusting. I could feel Lord Grey's eyes on me, a stare that ruffled my hair and set my teeth grinding. I'd never appreciated being watched.

I knelt to wipe under a squat bookcase and saw a blink of shine. Stretching out a hand, I gripped an object—a thick crystal, darkly colored on one side, as if smoke had seeped in.

"Sir?" I turned, cradling the object.

"Oh, good."

I handed it to him and bent to grab my duster.

"What did you do to it?" Lord Grey asked.

"Sir, I just picked it up. I did nothing to it."

Wonderful, I'd gone and broken it somehow. "Is it broken, sir?"

He kept staring at the cylinder of light, then at me. "Come here, Anne."

Bugger. "Yes, sir." He stretched out a hand and pulled a stone the color of moldy cheese from a nearby table.

"Hold this."

"Sir, I'd rather not. I'm afraid I'll break it."

"Just do it."

I opened my palm and he placed the stone inside. There was a sudden burning, like a drop of hot candle-wax, before the stone grew cold, the heat disappearing. The master took it back and breathed in sharply.

"Let me see your palm," he whispered.

I raised my hand.

"No, the other one." He pointed at my left hand, the one that had lain against the mirror the night before. Lord Grey's shining eyes traveled to my palm, where the dim outline of symbols could still be seen. He passed a hand through his hair.

"That's enough, Anne. Please leave."

"Of . . . of course, sir."

I left the room, my hand still held before me.

Dora was on the stairs waiting for me. I could see her tendrils of hair snaking around the banister as she moved.

"So, what did he want?"

I could not read her face, it was locked tight against me.

"A little tidying up." I attempted to pass by her, but she stepped in front of me, her eyes on my face.

"That's all? And why now, why you, after all these years?"

I shrugged. "You would have to ask Lord Grey."

Dora laughed. "Right." She slinked down the stairs like a bored cat, while I followed with my hand locked on the banister.

"Anne, listen. If I were you, I would not get too chummy with his highness up there," she said.

"For goodness' sake, Dora. I just cleaned his room, I'm not scheming to steal him away from you."

"From me? What could I bloody want with that stick?"

"I don't know. But you're acting strange."

"I'm telling you, it'd be wise to keep a wide berth from that man."

I sighed. "I'm getting tired of the hidden nonsense this household is keeping. What is going on? Is it some twisted idea of a test? An initiation into the manor?" My voice had swollen into a shout that bounced against the walls. I quieted down.

"Dora, I'm exhausted. My body aches with the constant cold, and nothing has made sense since I stepped foot in this house."

"I can't tell you anything, Anne. I'm not free to discuss it. None of us are."

My eyes narrowed. "So there is something to discuss?"

"Stay away from Lord Grey." Her cheeks had reddened in competition with her hair.

"Wonderful. I'm supposed to tell the master of the house to 'shove off' if he asks for me. Good advice." I passed by her, unwilling to continue a pointless conversation.

I went to my room, but the walls felt tight around me, as if they were leaning in, too tired to stand up straight. I jumped off the chair where I'd been resting and raced down the corridor toward the front door. No one stopped me.

The day was soaking with clouds that veiled the weak sun—a day for staying inside—but I would have rather been anywhere, even in the biting air, than inside the trap that was the manor.

Where could I go? Not to the fountain, and not around the other side unless I wanted to bleed to death, punctured by the black trees. I circled around, making loops before deciding to visit the stables. At the very least, I could greet my fellow travelers.

The large door opened with ease and no sound, and the musky odor, warm with sweat and cloying manure, pulled me in. The first two stalls were occupied by the horse duo I'd had the pleasure of meeting. They looked cozy in their mangers, their hooves pawing, noses snorting.

The next stall contained a table and chair, both made from wood that was rough and unwaxed. The bed in the corner was even cruder, with only a horse blanket the color of a mouse's pelt to cover the sleeper. Why would Mr. Keery choose to spend his nights in a barn stall rather than in a real room?

I looked around for him. As I stepped away from the gurgling horses, I began to hear a muted voice drifting from the last stalls, the ones cloaked in darkness. For some reason, my insides knotted at the sound. Despite the cold, sweat broke out on my forehead and my heart sped up in my chest. I didn't want to go further into the darkness, but I had to know what was hiding in those stalls. The voice got louder and louder as I moved down the dirt footpath, until I rounded the corner and swung the light door inward. It was Mr. Keery, talking in his sleep.

He was sitting on the floor, flanked by straw on every side, and leaning his head against the wall behind him. His hands grabbed at his clothes, pulling, and, as I watched, a contortion of muscles shook his wrinkled skin. He cried out in his sleep.

I wasn't sure I should wake him when he was dreaming that deeply, but I didn't want him to linger in whatever personal hell he was suffering through. I stepped close and hay snapped beneath my feet. He didn't notice. I placed a shaking hand on his arm and shook him with as much care as I could.

"Mr. Keery. Mr. Keery, wake up."

He moved, but did not open his eyes. A burnt odor breathed out of him. My skin rippled in something it understood, recognized, but that I refused to acknowledge.

"Mr. Keery."

His eyes flew open, but they were not the ones I was used to; these were deeper, darker. He gave me a smile that revealed all his poor teeth, while his breath came faster, as if he'd been running.

I gasped and leapt backward.

"Miss, are you all right?" Mr. Keery's voice sounded drunk with sleep, but normal. His eyes had returned to their tired blue.

"Oh, I'm fine. I thought I heard something. Sorry to bother you."

Before he got the opportunity to say anything, I rose and left the stables.

All right, one more odd occurrence, and one more place I did not want to visit again.

Even in the open air, I began to feel choked; I gave up on my afternoon walk and returned to the manor.

"Ms. Simple," I called as I heard her moving in the dining room.

"Yes, Anne?" She stopped wiping the furniture.

"I'm concerned about Mr. Keery."

"What about him?"

I sighed, rubbing my forehead in frustration. "He's not looking well. Have you not noticed? Has no one noticed? Just now, I saw him in the stables, talking in his sleep."

She was watching me from across the large table. I caught her hands pecking at each other, pinching her fingers' edges, but she stopped when she saw my eyes following them. With a sigh, she motioned for me to follow her.

What now? Would I finally get some answers?

FOURTEEN

MS. SIMPLE LED ME TO HER ROOM, WHICH WAS a wider version of my own and even boasted the luxury of a bookshelf. It was stark, however, the walls covered in beige paper, with the only adornment hanging over the bed—a plain crucifix swinging over her pillow.

"Please sit." She pointed to the only chair as she sat on the edge of her bed. In such a vulnerable position, with her hands tucked into the folds of her skirt, she looked like a girl in clothes much too big for her. I felt the sudden urge to hold her hand, to comfort her somehow.

"I am also concerned about Mr. Keery. I fear he may not last much longer."

I shifted my weight forward, my elbows on my knees. "We need to call for a doctor."

"We can't," she said.

"Of course we can. I can manage with the horses. I'll go to the nearest town and bring back someone to look at him."

"No, Anne. None of us can leave. And even if we could, I doubt anyone would come back to help Peter."

"Why do you say that?"

Ms. Simple rubbed her wrist, where I could see a vague dimpling of skin—deep puncture marks—the surrounding flesh chafed into a brown rawness.

"This house has seen more than its share of misfortune, and people are frightened to come near it. At first, it was just the superstitious that refused, but slowly, everyone has abandoned us to this endless isolation. It's hard to imagine, Anne, but at one point, years ago, every room was full and every bed held a warm body at night. A busy household, like any other. There were celebrations and music— Lord Grey's mother loved all that. Oh, the music that used to course along these walls! You wouldn't have recognized the young Lord either. He was a happy creature, especially when Miss Bellingham was around. They were so close." She nodded. "He was a different person with her, all smiles and kind words."

Miss Bellingham again. What had happened between them? I was about to ask when Ms. Simple continued, and I dared not interrupt.

"And then it all changed so suddenly. The young master left for London when he came of age, to study and pursue his many interests. But one winter, five years ago, he returned without warning, brimming with energy. As soon as he stepped foot in the manor, everything changed. He'd always been an excitable youth, but now, his energy was smothering. I would pass by him and feel myself overtaken, my insides spinning into nausea, my thoughts getting more and more confused. He had that effect on everyone, including his parents. There was a deep well of violent energy in that boy. It was difficult to be around him then, but it got worse after his mother died. Instead of normal grieving, the kind his father was dealing with, he kept himself aloof from everything and everyone. There were days when his bed was not slept in, and I would find him curled up around a book, his eyes wide and too bright.

"Soon after, things began to happen. Benign things at first: lights bursting on in the middle of the night, the stomping of sudden thunder vibrating through the house, things of that sort. His father intervened, to no avail."

"But what was Lord Grey *doing*? What caused all of those disturbances?" I asked.

"I'm not sure. I was never very close to Lord Grey. He always frightened me, even when he was a young boy. All I know is that things got much worse. One night, I was woken by the breaking of glass from the upstairs rooms. Half the household rushed to see what had happened, and we found the young master unconscious on a mattress of glass shards, cuts and bruises staining his body's every surface. The beginning of the end was gathered up along with those mirror shards. The cold slithered in and refused to leave, and on its tail, an even colder fear. That's when the first batch of servants gave notice, six in all. And that's when—"

Her voice sliced off and was replaced by a dull clap. My eyes widened as Ms. Simple's head jerked to the side. She raised a hand to her cheek.

"Ms. Simple! What is it?" I was by her side. Fear chilled me to the bone. The dread I'd felt (and chalked up to nerves), for the past three weeks was reflected in Ms. Simple's eyes. I pulled her hand away from her face, and saw the imprint of a large hand on her skin. It was a damp red, a painful rose against the snow of the housekeeper's face.

Ms. Simple did not want to say anything else after that, and I couldn't blame her. Something dark, a slug of night, was living between these walls, making life reach unbearable levels of fright. Lord Grey was involved, that was obvious, but how? And why?

The questions followed me through a tight dinner, the three of us women attempting to ignore Mr. Keery's feverish mumblings.

Dora flinched at Ms. Simple's cheek, but uttered no questioning word. The little conversation we could muster up between cold bites of beef stew was focused solely on housework.

"Did you get to the curtains in the study today, Anne?"

"Yes, Ms. Simple. I've already hung them back up."

"Wonderful. Tomorrow, begin with the library's."

"Of course, Ms. Simple."

After Dora and I washed the dishes, with not a single word lost between the two of us, I headed back to our quarters. Ms. Simple's door was ajar, so I crossed to it and knocked. Through the open slit, I saw her jump at the sound.

"I'm sorry, I didn't mean to startle you. I just wanted to see if you were all right," I said, opening the door completely.

From her red eyes, I could tell she'd been crying, but she gave me a small smile. I'd always been a weak one when it came to seeing grown people cry; all I wanted to do was soothe them back to normal.

"Do you need anything, Ms. Simple? Water? Tea, maybe?"

"No, thank you, Anne. You're very kind." She cleared her throat and gathered herself together. I watched as she brushed her eyes with a handkerchief, and then tucked it back into her pocket. Her hands were shaking badly enough to make that a difficult task. A sudden vision of my mother flooded my eyes, making my heart pound in surprise: my infant self watching her hands folding bedsheets as her tears fell onto the fabric. The sadness I'd felt then tumbled over me again. I blinked the memory away before it swallowed me.

"We'll find a way through this, Ms. Simple." Whatever *this* was.

She looked at me, her face dark and empty of hope. "I pray you're right, child. I just don't see how."

There was nothing else I could say; no other words I could give her that would comfort her.

"Goodnight, Ms. Simple."

She nodded. "Remember to bolt your door, Anne."

"Yes, thank you."

I closed her door and staggered to my room, my body and mind so heavy, I couldn't carry them much longer. As I sat on my bed, I wondered what could lie in store for the five of us.

FIFTEEN

A DIFFERENT NOISE WOKE ME THAT NIGHT: AN echo of what I imagined to be a growl bounced against my door, followed by the snap of splitting wood. Coughs filled the subsequent silence. Lord Grey.

There was not even a glimmer of light coming from the window, so I couldn't have slept for more than a few hours. The exhaustion I felt as I moved confirmed my guess. I put my shoes on with my eyes still half-closed, ungluing them felt like too much of an effort, and thanked the Lord that I hadn't had the energy to undress.

A crash, the crackling of china, succeeded in jolting me into action, and I hurried to my door. There was no light in the hall, no sound from the rooms around me. Walking into the empty hallway, I moved down it and to the kitchen. From under the door, I caught a line of candle-glow and, with it, a trickle of sound.

I opened the door and looked in.

Lord Grey was kneeling, picking up the scraps of a broken teacup lying on the floor. For all his height, he looked so small crouching there. The teacup had been flung across the room from the china cabinet and had smashed into pieces so small, the force used on it must have been incredible. One of the chairs was also destroyed, splintered out of almost all recognition. Could the slight man before me have done that? He lifted his eyes as I stepped forward.

"Sir, leave it. I'll do it." I knelt next to him and reached to take the china from his hands. He flinched.

"I'd prefer if you didn't touch me, Anne."

I blinked. What?

He rose and threw what he held in his hands into the dust bin, picking shards off his palm with care.

"I think it might not be a bad thing, Anne, if you stayed away from me."

"Sir, why?"

"I will not be held responsible for what might happen."

"Sir, what do you mean? What could happen?"

His laugh was too dark to be comforting. "Anything, Anne. Anything."

He left the room. A flare of warmth ran through me; it was not right, not fair. I deserved to know what was occurring around me. I chased after Lord Grey, questions bubbling in my mouth, regardless of their propriety or lack thereof. He turned at my steps.

"Sir, I'm sorry, I don't want to overstep my bounds, but I'd really appreciate knowing the truth of what's happening in the manor."

"You don't need to know. At least, not yet."

"If I am to stay, I think I deserve to understand what I'm choosing."

His body oozed black hostility.

"The door is open. Leave whenever you like."

"No, sir, I will not abandon my post."

"Your post? That's what you're concerned about? I'll write you a glowing letter of reference, don't worry." He laughed. His chest rose as a coughing spell overtook him.

I waited until the spasm passed. "What else should I be concerned about?"

He stepped toward me in the night-filled hall.

"Your life."

Lord Grey turned again, heading for the stairs, but I reached out and grasped his arm. Me and my damn hands.

A jolt raced up my palm, numbing my fingers and wrist, making me jerk my hand back with a yelp.

"Not the wisest thing to do."

I looked up into his face, afraid of what I'd find, but his eyes were as still and quiet as always. Nothing flickered behind their stare.

"Let me see." He gathered an edge of his shirt and wrapped it around his hand so that no bare skin remained. He then extended the cloth-wrapped appendage toward me, but I pressed my injured hand with my left one and shook my head.

"I don't think so, sir."

With an impatient release of air, he yanked my hand toward him with a stronger grip than I would have imagined. I felt no new pain at his touch, but my palm's numbness had begun to fade, leaving behind a trail of hot thorns.

"I did warn you, if you recall. It's a minor burn, nothing to sob over, but I'm sure it hurts."

I nodded.

"Come, I have something to help with the pain." He released my hand and headed for the stairs.

Against all reason, I followed.

Lord Grey lit all the lights in his antechamber, giving the room a comforting glow, a square of light amid the pressing darkness. Then he glanced through one of his cabinets stocked full of jars with different colored pastes and powders.

"Here, put this on your hand." He unscrewed the lid of a little round container and passed it to me. It smelled sweet, yet spicy, a hint of pepper tickling my nose.

"What is it, sir?"

"It's a balm for burns."

My face must have betrayed my skepticism, because he chuckled. "It's not poison."

I dipped a finger in the cool cream and spread it on my pulsing palm. I gasped as the salve seemed to gather the pain to it, erasing it from my hand.

"Yes, it's quite good. My own creation."

I handed the jar back to him, careful not to graze his skin with any part of mine. I didn't know why, or how, he'd burned me, but I did know I didn't want to experience it again.

He turned away from me to close and lock the cabinet behind him. As the lock clicked in place with the dry turn of a key, Lord Grey spoke:

"I suppose I should begin with the roses, with how I created them. It's the most logical place to start . . . maybe the only place."

I shook my head. "Sir, what do you mean, *you* created them? You planted them?"

"No. That is not what I mean. I thought them into being."

I blinked, the words still not making sense. "How is that possible, sir?"

His thin shoulders shrugged. "How can someone sing, or draw, or play the piano? It's an ability I was born with and that I've nurtured, but I think you're not as foreign to this type of thing as you're letting on."

I opened my mouth, but he waved my words away with a sharp hand.

"It doesn't matter."

Lord Grey's hands twined around each other. The words he had already shared with me seemed to have erased some of the weary marks off his face—his brows were relaxed, his forehead smooth. He looked rather handsome.

The thought took me by surprise, making me blush in the lamplight.

"You don't believe me," Lord Grey said.

"Sir, I would never question your words."

"But you don't believe me."

I took a breath. "Sir, it just seems unlikely."

Without shifting his eyes off of me, Lord Grey exhaled, once, and my knowledge of the world tilted, never to be righted again.

The chair next to me, trembling with books, slid across the floor, not even a single book shifting in surprise.

"What just happened?"

"I made the chair move." He said it with such lightness, such boredom, that I began laughing. Loud hiccups of hard laughter traveled up my body, shaking me from head to foot.

"Are you quite finished, Anne?"

I wiped my eyes, attempting to also wipe away what I'd witnessed. "Sir, I need to see it again."

He rolled his eyes. "Fine."

Without warning, the chair scurried back to its place.

My eyes were about to slip out of their sockets.

"If we are quite done with the demonstrations, I would like to continue. Sit." His words were seeping with irritation. I wasn't sure I had any words left.

"If it's all the same, sir, I'd rather not."

"Sit."

I obeyed without another moment's hesitation.

I placed the thick books on the floor and sat with care on the richly upholstered seat. He remained standing, fiddling with a loose string from his shirt cuff for an instant, then headed for one of the overburdened bookshelves. With only the slightest sign of hesitation, he plucked something from behind a pile of books and walked back to where I sat. He opened his hand, holding up the object: a small, perfectly round, silver mirror.

"Please don't touch it, Anne. I'd rather not have to replace this, if at all possible. Can you see into it clearly?"

My face looked back at me, my dark eyes wide and my skin pale. "Yes, sir."

"Good. Now pay attention, I'll only do this once."

He said one more word, one I couldn't understand, and everything around me was swallowed by darkness. Everything except for the mirror, which glittered more than anything I'd ever seen before, more than any jewels any Lady could ever buy.

"Look in, Anne," Lord Grey said.

I did.

Rosewood Manor rose in front of me, resplendent in the morning light. I blinked. How had I gotten here? How was it morning already?

I turned, hoping to spy some clue from my surroundings, but nothing explained what I was doing out here, when I'd just been in Lord Grey's chambers.

Nor why all the roses were gone.

They were conspicuous in their absence, the red blooms which I'd grown so used to seeing and smelling. Actually, the entire manor looked different. Younger. But that wasn't possible.

The front door opened without warning, and out came a woman dressed in a gown the color of lavender sprigs, her dark hair pinned in a perfect bun on her head. Behind her, his face turned up to her as if she were the very sun, was a small boy. He couldn't have been more than six or seven, but one glance told me who he was. I held my breath.

It was Lord Grey. That boy was the man with whom I'd just been sitting.

"Come, August," the woman said. Her eyes passed over me as she looked down the long carriageway. "Your father is almost here." She stretched out a hand and the boy took it, the smile on his face so bright it seemed to radiate outward. "Let's see what he's brought you for your birthday, my darling."

The boy looked out as well, his eyes resting on me for just an instant, his brow furrowing with curiosity. But the unmistakable sound of a carriage pulled his eyes away.

"He's here!" August cried, leaping into the air in excitement. The air around him shivered with his energy, with his absolute glee.

That was when it happened: the roses, all of them, all the ones I'd seen since the moment I had arrived at Rosewood, appeared. They rose up from the bare ground, from the many planted bushes, from in between the stone steps leading to the door.

The woman gasped, but August's eyes never wavered from where his father's carriage would be appearing.

"August," she said. "Oh, my darling." She brought a hand to her mouth and knelt down beside him. Her skin blushed in pale imitation of the flowers all around her, and her laugh wove itself around me much like the roses' scent.

The horses' hooves drew nearer and nearer, until we could all see the carriage and the two men who rode it—the coachman, a large man with drooping skin, and a man who could not have been anyone but August's father. His face was harsher, his eyes dark as oak, but I could see the resemblance in the way he moved as he opened the carriage door.

His smile dimmed, then disappeared.

"Jane, what in God's name?"

"He made them grow, William!"

"Who did? What are you talking about?"

"Our son did this!" She laughed. "He's our little wonder!"

August's father shook his head, fear etched clearly on his face.

There was a sudden soft peal, almost like Lady Caldwell's bell, and the scene around me froze. The day's light started to ebb, quickly contracting into a small circle on which only I stood. Then, even that vanished.

I reached a hand out to steady myself and felt fine linen against my palm. I opened eyes I hadn't realized I'd closed and looked about.

There were young men all around, fourteen or fifteen years old, their tailored suits belying their uncombed hair and rumpled shirts.

It was a large space, with two rows of beds spanning the room's length. A boy's dormitory, I realized. My cheeks warmed as that knowledge reached my head. What would Father say if he saw me here, surrounded by young men in various stages of undress?

Like before, no one seemed to see me as I edged around one of the beds, passing two young men washing their faces at the numerous white basins left between the rows of beds for just such a purpose.

"It happened again, August," the young man on the left said, bringing me to a stop. I turned so that I faced them, only the basins separating me from their image. There was Lord Grey. He looked less like the boy I'd just seen beaming at his mother and more like the man he'd become, someone too pale, too thin, someone who had forgotten what happiness felt like.

"It's a good thing I get up early, or you'd be thrown out of the school," the young man said. "What is happening? How are you doing it?"

Lord Grey shook his head. "I don't know, William. I didn't even know it was occurring until you told me." His eyes moved through the room, making sure no one could hear their conversation. As his gaze landed on me, he frowned. "What—"

But the boy next to him grabbed his arm, pulling his attention away from where I stood. "You didn't just rearrange the chairs this time, August. I could put up with that, or knocking things over, ripping our notes to shreds; they're all inconveniences, but manageable." He shook his head. "You set the curtains on fire. We could have been killed if I hadn't woken up."

Lord Grey's thin face lost the little bit of color it had. I feared he might collapse right there, without me being able to do anything about it. It was a surprisingly painful thought.

"I'm sorry, August. I will have to say something to the Headmaster about this. You are my friend, and I feel terrible about doing it, but you are putting all our lives in danger."

Lord Grey flinched as if burned. He swallowed and looked up to where I stood again. "I understand."

The same peal rang out from somewhere around me as the room shifted, blurring.

I was in another room, smaller but visibly wealthier. Every piece of furniture was polished to a high shine, every cushion fluffed up and positioned perfectly on the armchairs next to me. The large windows let in swaths of light and a view of London that made my breath catch in my throat.

I recognized Lord Grey at once this time, even though he had his back turned to me. He sat at a desk, his head bent to read the book in front of him as an older man looked on. He looked like every other tutor I'd ever seen: drab suit, crooked glasses sliding down his nose, a thick book in his hands, and the bored gaze of someone who had said the same things over and over until they held no mystery anymore.

In a second, all of that changed.

As with the roses, the air trembled around Lord Grey for an instant and then the tutor was no longer holding a book, but a large toad. The poor man gasped, dropping the croaking animal to the gleaming floorboards.

Lord Grey lifted his head. "Sir, I didn't mean to."

"But you did do it?" There was an eagerness in his voice that made me frown. I walked forward so that I could see both his and Lord Grey's faces clearly.

"Yes, sir."

The tutor stepped closer to the desk and pointed to the ink pen resting by the opened book. "Move that," he said.

Lord Grey reached out.

"No, without touching it."

When Lord Grey hesitated, the tutor placed his hands on the desk and bent forward. "Do it," he ordered.

The young man before me, someone who wasn't much older than the boy I'd just seen in the dormitory, closed his eyes, his brow furrowing with effort. Long seconds passed in which the only movement was the rise and fall of both men's chests as they breathed.

Suddenly, the pen jerked forward, careening off the desk. Lord Grey lay back, panting.

The tutor smiled. "Good. Now, come with me."

"But my uncle—"

"Never mind your uncle."

The bell rang again and the room changed, the walls disappearing until I found myself outside, standing next to Lord Grey and the tutor as they waited to cross a busy London street.

"Follow me, August. Do *not* lose sight of me."

The man took off down a street so full of people, it took only a moment for me to lose him in the crowd. But not Lord Grey. He was already tall enough to see beyond my line of vision and, with a deep sigh, he started after him. I made sure to keep him in view.

I had no idea how many streets we took, how many people we jostled past, how much of London we saw, but Lord Grey always managed to stay just a few steps behind the older man. The streets became alleyways, and the people around us were no longer dressed in finery, but in various stages of poverty, until rags were the only things to be seen. Rats scurried between our feet and harsh laughter mingled with screams, but Lord Grey continued walking, never wavering.

At last, the tutor stopped before a dilapidated door stained with suspicious colors which I did not care to investigate further.

"Do not utter a word until I say so," the tutor said as he brought up a hand and knocked once on the door.

Lord Grey nodded and, curiously, turned to where I stood, lifting an eyebrow in question. Could he see me? No, that was impossible. But, then again, all of this was impossible.

The door opened without a sound and a man as finely dressed as any London Lord peered out. His eyes moved from the tutor to Lord Grey. He stepped aside and allowed us in.

"We're here to see the Master," the tutor said when the door closed behind us. "It's urgent."

The man nodded. "Please, wait here."

The room was full of men of all ages, all dressed in the most expensive cuts and fabrics, all of them holding round glasses with amber liquid swirling at the bottom. Brandy, I assumed, even though it was noon, at most.

The younger men turned toward us as soon as we'd walked in, their eyes landing on Lord Grey, taking in his clothes, his apparent wealth, his age.

As we waited, I took in the room. There were no windows, and shadows piled all around us; the smell of tobacco, sweet and dark like coffee, filled every nook. I began to feel trapped, the room bending close around me so that I had to place a hand on the wall to keep my balance. I had no idea what would happen if I fainted, but I didn't want to find out.

"Gareth, how wonderful to see you," a man walking toward us said. I hadn't noticed him and from Lord Grey's flinch, he hadn't either.

He was older than most of the other men. A collection of wrinkles, there was a crown of white down circling his head, the pale skin beneath it almost glowing in the candlelight. His eyes were clear pools, with only a tinge of blue. But despite his benign look, there was an aura of strength around him that made my skin prickle in the warm room.

"Master, the pleasure is mine," the tutor said with a nod. "This is August Grey, a young man with the kind of abilities I think are of interest to you."

The Master's eyes turned. "Lord Grey, what an honor. I was not aware your estimable father possessed a child with the talents in which I focus."

"Sir, what talents?"

"If your tutor has brought you here, then you, son, possess remarkable abilities, of which I'm sure you are aware."

Lord Grey frowned and turned to his tutor. "Is this about what happened this morning?"

"Yes, August. And what I assume has been happening for quite some time." He turned back to the Master. "His father hired me after Crandell Academy expelled him for some unexplained incidents. I must admit, I was curious to see if he had any of our skills, but it still took me by surprise when I saw evidence of them this morning."

"Is this true, son?"

"Yes, sir."

"Yes, I can see how they would." He leaned forward and held the young man's gaze. "Would you like to learn how to control them?"

The bells rang in my head and abruptly, I was in another room, one with three men standing in front of a long, tall, laboratory table. Another man, one with sunset-red hair, stood at the room's head.

A spell of dizziness overtook me. Every shift in location was becoming harder to bear.

"To be in The Order of Brothers," the red-haired man said, "you must learn how to manipulate the elements, how to make them bend to your will. To have gotten this far in the training, all three of you have shown enormous natural talents, but it is not over yet. A magician's training is never done."

Magician? He couldn't be talking about sleight-of-hand, but it was preposterous to think he meant real magic. My head pounded with doubt.

"Today, only one of you will step forward as a true magician worthy of joining The Order." His eyes traveled from one man to another, lingering for just a second on Lord Grey's face. "You may begin."

Lord Grey stood at one end of the table, his body completely still. I stood next to him and watched his hands clench with effort. The other two men at the table were all shifting about, muttering strange words to themselves, making peculiar symbols in the air with shaking fingers. But not young Lord Grey.

Standing next to him, the energy was like a boiling pot of water. Heat brushed my face and hands, as if it called to me, pulling something in my very center forward. My entire body wanted to walk closer to him, put my hands on his. The impulse was strong enough to frighten me.

Next to me, Lord Grey's eyes shifted toward me again, just for an instant. I backed away from the table.

It took seconds for an orb of fire to appear in Lord Grey's thin hands. It was so bright, I couldn't stare at it for too long without my eyes watering, though the other men were transfixed by its light. My hands started shaking. How was this happening?

"Well done, Grey," the red-haired man said. "A perfect specimen." He barely glanced at the other two men. "I've never seen someone so young conjure one up. Your talent is obvious." He smiled a thin smile. "Welcome to The Order of Brothers."

I was jerked forward with no warning this time, no sound or dimming lights, and deposited once again next to Lord Grey, but this time outside. He was dressed in his finest, standing beside a young woman in a luscious gown. Her face was resplendent in the gaslights around where we stood. A theater, I guessed, by the building's size.

"Oh, August, it was lovely, thank you," she said with a glittering laugh.

"Anything to please you, Miss Bellingham."

"Please, it's Lilly."

Lilly Bellingham. The Lilly Elsie had mentioned?

Lord Grey's head turned suddenly to where I stood. He gently shook his head.

The scene disappeared again. Nausea roiled up and down my stomach until I thought I'd be ill. This was getting to be too much for me. When I could trust I wouldn't stain my shoes with my supper, I looked up.

Lord Grey stood tall in front of the Master, his pale face tight with anger. "I am seventeen years old, sir. I will make up my own mind."

"But why do you wish to leave the order?"

"Sir, my reasons are not important."

"That remains to be seen, son."

Lord Grey's jaw tightened. "I don't see why it is anyone's concern, but if it will end this nonsense sooner, then I will tell you, sir. I feel I have learned all I can from my teachers and fellow students, and I see the necessity of ending my affiliation."

"But you are a talented young man, or so your teachers say. Why choose to finish your studies in this art?"

"Sir, you misunderstand me. I will continue my studies, outside of the order."

The Master's lips thinned. "I see." He cleared his throat. "Well, then, there's little else for us to discuss."

Lord Grey nodded. "Then I will take my leave, sir. Please give Miss Bellingham my compliments."

The Master knew Miss Bellingham?

The older man lifted a finger. "One moment, I just recalled that tomorrow is a ritual day."

"Yes, sir, but what does that have to do with me, now?"

"As you know, we need at least fifteen members to make a ritual day successful, and I'm afraid you will have to attend to complete the set tomorrow."

"What about one of the provisional members?"

"They are both out of the country. And, as you know, we cannot allow the uninitiated to do anything but observe. It would only be a couple of hours, after which you'd be free to leave our company. It's a favor you'd be granting us, otherwise, we'll be forced to postpone the celebration."

There was something in his voice that made me shiver as he looked at Lord Grey. I wished I could tell him to leave, to take the hat on the desk and walk out of the room.

Lord Grey sighed. "As you wish. I'll remain until tomorrow."

I staggered and grabbed on to the nearest thing, which just happened to be Lord Grey's black robe. Someone's elbow struck my side, pushing me against the dark wall behind me and forcing me to let go of Lord Grey's sleeve.

We were in yet another dark room. The smell of incense was overpowering, though by now, my nausea was so strong a brisk wind could have set it off. The room was full of men, the majority of them wearing the same black robes Lord Grey wore, a red cross surrounded by a circle sewn into the left sleeves—the order's emblem.

There was an entire row of men at the back, however, who were dressed in wealthy men's everyday waistcoats. They had to be the uninitiated, the ones who would only be allowed to watch.

Lord Grey sighed next to me.

"August," a middle-aged man said, walking up to both of us. "I didn't know you'd be here. I heard rumors you were leaving us."

"I am, Allister. This will be my last ceremony. I will be returning to Rosewood tomorrow."

"That is a shame, son. Your talent is extraordinary."

More and more men stepped into the room, though only two more wore robes. Lord Grey seemed to follow my gaze.

"I thought Jonathan and Walter were out of the country."

"So did I."

Lord Grey turned to the room's center, where the Master stood, waiting for the men to finish entering. The old man's face had no expression.

A door slammed shut behind us, and I winced.

"Welcome, Brothers," the Master began, motioning for the men to arrange themselves into what appeared to be their usual circle. "We are here to celebrate the art, the power that has brought us all together, that has brought us into the light of knowledge, that has revealed our superiority over the common man."

Lord Grey stepped forward to join the other members in the circle.

"For the edification of the uninitiated, this ritual is performed every season to awaken our minds to the changes around us, and to attune ourselves to each other once again. In this room, at this time, we are true Brothers." He paused. "However. Tonight, there is another matter to discuss before we begin our celebration. August Grey, please step forward."

Lord Grey's head snapped to attention. He looked around the circle as I did, meeting only completely blank faces. Even Allister shrugged.

He stepped forward.

"This member of our order has decided to abscond his duties," the Master said. "A pity."

The room appeared to hold its breath. One of the men behind Lord Grey stepped forward and shoved him to his knees before I even had the chance to understand what was happening.

"He thinks he is too smart, too talented to remain with us. He thinks he has surpassed our abilities."

Laughter seemed to swarm around the room as Lord Grey stood, once again, to face the Master.

"Let us see if his power matches his arrogance."

As his last words dimmed, a monstrous chanting began, guttural and harsh, expanding in the very air we breathed. The temperature plummeted as the candles petered out, leaving us all in absolute blackness.

For long moments, there was nothing; no sound, not even the breathing of the men I knew were still in the room. The cold was an agony. I turned around to look for any glimmer of light, trying to tear through the darkness around me, when I heard Lord Grey groan.

"Sir!" I cried, without concern for anyone else hearing me. There was another groan, but I didn't know where he was. I needed to get to him!

I saw the eyes at the same time Lord Grey did, for we gasped in unison. They were a blinding yellow, glowing enough to allow me vision, but before I could take advantage of it, something lifted Lord Grey high into the air and flung him across the room. He crashed against the floor with a crack of bones.

None of the men went to his aid. Someone had to help him!

I tried to slip into the circle, but a jolt of heat pushed me back, just like when I'd touched Lord Grey's hand. I tried again as whatever creature the Brothers had summoned hissed and stalked after its prey, but all I managed was to burn myself. The creature's eyes got closer and closer to the crumpled figure on the floor.

"Someone do something! Sir!" I screamed.

As if he'd heard me, Lord Grey lifted his head, catching sight of what was hunting him. He shouted something I couldn't understand and a pool of light surrounded him. Stumbling to his feet, he reeled as far away from the eyes as he could manage. The circle held him trapped inside, like it held me outside, the men stoic in absolute silence.

"Sir, look out!" I screamed just as the air rippled next to him. Lord Grey leapt aside at the last second, missing a strike by a hair's width. Had he heard me?

Fear tightened around me, as I was sure it tightened around him. He had to know what to do to end this. He was a magician, one of the Brothers!

Lord Grey looked in my direction and I could see, even from that distance, how frightened he was.

"Do something, sir," I said, my voice cutting through the darkness. I knew he survived; he was sitting in his chambers with me this very second, showing me his life, but it was all so real. He didn't need me to do this; I knew that as well, since I hadn't been there the first time, when this had really happened. So why did I feel so powerless, like I'd failed him at the most crucial of moments?

Lord Grey turned back to the creature I still couldn't see, facing it even as its growls sent chills down my spine. He lifted his arms high above his head and held them there.

I began to hear gasps and the screams of splitting wood. Warmth spread out around me, rising to a boil, morphing the air before my eyes into a shimmering curtain.

Lord Grey's voice sliced through the sudden noise, power coiled in his every syllable.

"Get thee gone!" he screamed and slammed his arms down to his side.

All air left the room as the explosion ripped through it. I was thrown backward against the wall, screams rising from all around me to an unbearable level. I covered my head as objects crashed on top of me, burying me under their painful weight, and waited for the end, whatever that might mean.

Seconds, minutes, or even hours later, I became aware that the screams had stopped, and that nothing was collapsing on me anymore. Shifting my arms, I allowed the rubble that covered me to slide off my body. My limbs ached, but I wasn't bleeding, not that I could see, at least.

The room, however, was scored with red. Blood covered the floorboards, glittering like ink in the light that had suddenly returned, pooling around each body.

Oh, Lord, the bodies!

Every man who'd been in the room was dead. The Master, Allister, all the uninitiated. Their bodies lay in the most impossible of angles, their flesh torn at the most vicious places.

Lord Grey lay in the middle of the circle, immobile.

"Sir," I whispered and scrambled toward him. "Sir!"

But I was being pulled backward even as my hands dug into the boards to hold on to this moment. I needed to see what was going to happen to him, what would happen to all these people, but it was already rushing away from me, the room changing.

I gasped as Rosewood's sitting room appeared before me, Lord Grey looking thinner than ever, his eyes unrecognizable as he paced back and forth.

"You need help, August," his father said. "You need to sleep. To see a doctor. You haven't rested for a moment since you've returned. What happened in London, son?"

"Leave me alone! Just leave me be!"

The memories shifted faster now, faster than I could grasp.

Lord Grey pacing for hours in his chambers, his hands trembling with energy, his eyes half-mad with thoughts too dark to begin to guess at; Ms. Simple appearing, pushing plates of food toward him, picking them up untouched hours later; Lady Grey, the woman I'd seen in lavender, coughing her way to the grave as her son looked on from the pool of shadows in which he lived; Lord Grey ripping a letter to shreds while his father watched, the only visible words left, *Lilly Bellingham*; Lord Grey turning to books, thick tomes of unfamiliar symbols opening up before him, his hands landing on pages at random, calling out words as if they were his salvation; creatures rising from nothing, from air, objects appearing and disappearing, fires started and snuffed out with a single glance from feverish eyes.

Just as I thought I wouldn't be able to stand any more, the flashes stopped.

Lord Grey sat in his room with a book opened before him.

"Sir, please," I said just as he opened his own mouth. A string of complicated, twisted syllables left his lips.

I knew what had happened as soon as the cold entered the room. I recognized the chill, the kind that invaded every piece of flesh it touched. It was the same chill I'd been fighting since I'd stepped foot in Rosewood Manor.

It had no real shape, shifting between male and female, animal and human, visible and invisible without care. Lord Grey watched it with a thin smile on his face.

"Do you think you're strong enough to kill me?" he asked. "I welcome your attempts." He opened his thin arms and closed his eyes. "No? Well, that is a shame." He brought his arms down as he had in the order's room, and I braced myself for another disaster.

Nothing happened.

The creature laughed. I gasped at the familiar sound, feeling the hairs on my arms prickling with fear.

"Oh, August, my boy, you think I'll make it so simple for you? No. You did not pay attention in class, it seems. Your skills are not enough. They will never be enough."

With that, the creature lunged at him and lifted him off the floor.

"And do you know why, dear August?" It growled softly. "Because I am a part of you. I will feed off you until the day you die, and there is nothing you can do about it."

It released its grip and Lord Grey crashed to the floor.

I gasped as the round mirror disappeared from before me.

"Take a moment, Anne. It was a lot of information for you to process, but it's better to see it all at once. There is just a bit more I'd like you to understand, but I thought it best to let you come back to the present for a moment."

Words had abandoned me. My head throbbed with everything I'd seen and felt, with everything the man sitting in front of me had lived through. I opened my mouth to speak, but my mouth was so dry I had to clear it a handful of times before anything but a croak came out.

"It can't be true, sir," I said.

"I can assure you, it is. All of it."

I rubbed a hand across my aching forehead. "Magic exists? Demons and creatures, it's all real, sir?" He nodded. "That's what haunting this house?"

"I'm afraid so."

"But, sir, you were able to . . . kill the demon the order conjured up."

"The term is 'banish.'"

"Banish, then, sir. You were able to do so then, why can't you with this one? Is it because of what the creature said, that it is a part of you, sir?"

Lord Grey looked away. "Partly. The creature I conjured is a wraith, a powerful being, much more powerful than the demon the order set loose against me. It feeds off my energy, making it impossible for me to banish it on my own. And there is one other thing I need to know before I can attempt to defeat it: who its master is."

"But sir, if you called it up, shouldn't it serve you? Shouldn't you be its master?"

Lord Grey's eyes pierced mine. "That's the very question I've asked myself over and over since all of this began. You see, demons dwell in an in-between space that even magicians know nothing about. They are wild and untrained, but can be called up for short amounts of time to perform specific orders, as the one the Master raised against me was. It was no more than an animal, a large, powerful one, to be sure, but an animal nonetheless. Wraiths, however, roam our world, doing the bidding of their human masters. They are intelligent, familiar with our ways, able to manipulate us with one word. These creatures cannot just appear unbidden. That means someone conjured it before I did, since it is painfully obvious it does not recognize my authority. And yet, it came when I called it. A demon who is already bound to a human will not obey another's call unless it's ordered to do so. And since I do not know whom it serves, I cannot fully defeat it. All I would manage to do would be to cast it out for a while, but it would return, twice as strong."

"Do you have no suspicions as to who could have conjured it, sir?"

"Of course. The Master is my first choice; he was powerful enough to perform the conjuration, but as soon as he breathed his last in that room with the rest of the Brothers, his bond with the wraith would have cracked in two. Besides, Anne, you must remember that I called its name at random. No one sent it here. Its master could be anywhere in the world."

I frowned. This was all so confusing. Taking a breath, I steered Lord Grey back to the past, to what he did know. "And your father, sir? What happened to him?"

"He drowned. In the very fountain where you almost lost your life, Anne. He wasn't supposed to touch it, no human was, and he knew it all too well. The fountain was a kind of truce the wraith established with me, its home, of sorts. It promised not to harm the people I cared about, drawing its energy only from me and the fountain, as long as no one touched the black monstrosity." He sighed. "I did my best to warn them all, to keep them safe. You saw the symbols on the hall stones, all of them stamped there by my magic to offer what little protection I could grant. The mirror in the dining room, the same. But all my efforts were like holding a cloth napkin to stave off a thunderstorm. The wraith broke its promise and attacked my father as he sat in a drunken stupor, clawed at him in a frenzy of blades until it forced him out of the manor and into the surrounding woods."

My heart grew a layer of ice. "Sir, where was your father sitting when the attack began?"

"In the armchair in the sitting room, why?"

"I think I saw the marks."

He stopped moving. "You saw the claw marks."

I nodded. "As I was cleaning, sir."

His shoulders twitched in a shiver. "Yes, of course. That is why I keep the sheets on the furniture. Unpleasant, isn't it?"

"Yes, it is, sir."

"My father found himself at the foot of the fountain." Lord Grey's voice had thinned and paled. "Who knows what happened? Perhaps he staggered and reached for support, perhaps he was pushed. I found him later that day, bloated with water, his eyes reflecting the black marble underneath their dead gaze. That was almost six years ago."

I swallowed. "Sir, please forgive my presumption, but why have you all remained here? Surely leaving would have ended the nightmare," I said.

He shook his head. "No, I cannot leave. I am not allowed off the grounds."

"But Ms. Simple, Mr. Keery, and Dora? Why can't they leave?"

"The wraith does not allow the women off the grounds. They know too much already. Mr. Keery, though . . . you've seen what he's like. He is not a free man. The creature has sunk its claws deeply into him."

"But sir, how can it prevent you all from leaving?"

He sighed in irritation. "I'm not lying to you, Anne. You've felt it yourself when it attacked you on the stairs. If the creature wanted to stop us, to kill us even, it would."

"But to live in this fear . . ."

I couldn't even imagine waking to the seeping cold day after day for years. I'd only been in the manor a few weeks, and I feared I would never feel warm again.

"It was never quite this horrible. We had to watch our words and remain in the house, but for the most part, the five of us managed. That's why I wrote to Lady Caldwell to request a maid. She was the only one I still had a tepid contact with in the outside world. Things had quieted down into a sort of routine, so I could consider hiring someone to help Ms. Simple and Dora. I was wrong, as I tend to be when it comes to this creature.

"The day the letter arrived announcing your appointment, the cook was dragged from her bed and clawed to unconsciousness. I should have realized the danger, I should have sent a note immediately to prevent you from coming, but I didn't. I sent the coach three weeks later instead, to scoop you out of safety and into this frozen nightmare."

I looked at Lord Grey's face, at the youth and strength that lay hidden beneath layers of ashen worry and pale guilt.

"Sir, you couldn't have known."

His lips curled. "Right. That the wraith allowed the coach to fetch you should have been warning enough. It wanted you here, within its reach."

There was a moment of heavy silence before a thought made me speak.

"Sir, do you think it would have behaved this way with anyone who had taken my place, or is it me in particular who's causing all these tantrums?"

A genuine smile filled his face. "Tantrums. I like that, that's exactly what they are." He placed a hand in one of his pockets and brought out the smoky crystal I'd retrieved from under the bookshelf. He raised it to my eyes.

"Do you know what this is?"

"A crystal, sir."

"Do you know what it's for?"

"No, sir."

He shifted it, so the light from one of the lamps could play against its surface.

"This is a type of container. It stored energy so it could be accessed in a hurry. A last resort for an exhausted magician. I have two or three of these lying about, but I'd lost sight of this one until you found it . . . and broke it."

"Sir, honest, I didn't—"

"You didn't mean to do it, Anne, but you did. Just by touching it."

"I don't understand, sir."

"It's not an easy thing to explain. I'd never encountered it myself, although, I have heard about it. I began to suspect when the mirror in the dining room reacted with such violence to your touch."

"What? What did you suspect?"

"That you were not normal. That there was a seed of power in you, waiting to crack through its casing. And then the crystal proved it. Let me explain: a regular person would have picked it up without damage to herself or to the crystal, and neither of them would have been the worse for wear. If a magician held it, her energy would substitute the one already inside, but the crystal would not have been damaged. When you touched it, however, you erased the energy that slept inside it. You smothered it, like an errant fire. The crystal is worthless now."

Somewhere deep inside me, a chime rang, a note of dawning comprehension. I closed my eyes and listened.

"Anne," Lord Grey continued, "you are something different. A rare being, even rarer than a magician. You are the opposite—you are a Grounder."

I inhaled deeply. "A what, sir?"

"A Grounder. You harness energy and neutralize it. I think you have an inkling of what I'm talking about."

"But, sir, that's absurd. I've never done anything special, nothing that was not normal."

He leaned forward, his hands on the chair in front of him, and held my eyes. "Nothing strange has ever happened to you?"

I opened my mouth to assure him of that, but a vision of black feathers on snow, of translucent wings collapsing in shimmering heaps filled my eyes.

"Some birds . . . fell . . . around me. And moths." I gripped my trembling hands together.

"Ah," Lord Grey said. "You erased their power to fly."

"But I did nothing to cause it! I didn't even realize what was happening!"

"It doesn't matter. Your power is untrained, like mine was, and it strikes out as it wishes, with or without your consent."

"But that happened recently, I'd never experienced it before."

"Our powers develop as they like, when they like. It's possible that yours lay curled inside you, waiting for the right moment to emerge. Waiting until you were ready to accept them and use them as you should."

And the right moment had been while I cleared snow in Caldwell House's courtyard? No, perhaps whatever abilities I possessed had known I'd be sent here, to Rosewood. The thought made my stomach churn.

"What you are is also why my skin burns your own, you know. We are true opposites."

I shrugged. "Well, I don't know what to do with any of it, sir."

"You'll learn to wield the power soon enough."

"I don't want to learn. I want to leave it alone."

"Anne, have you heard nothing of what I've shared with you?"

I huffed. "I've heard plenty. I think you are not the best example to follow."

My eyes widened as the words left my mouth. Bugger.

Lord Grey turned his head and eyed me like a suspicious lizard.

"Hmm. Good thing I need you."

My voice was dry. "Need me, sir? Why?"

"You're going to help me banish this wraith."

SIXTEEN

HE REFUSED TO SAY ANYTHING ELSE ON THE subject.

"I'm exhausted, Anne, and by the looks of those charming bruises under your eyes, I suspect you are also. I think we should both try to get some rest."

I stood. A quake of dizziness shook me, and I grabbed on to the chair behind me. Lord Grey watched me with narrowed eyes, but did not attempt to help me. It was irritating to admit he was right; if I didn't sink down into sleep I would not make it through whatever the day's long hours held in store.

"Go rest, Anne. The last thing I need is you collapsing."

"Yes, sir. Is my room safe? I've been bolting the door at night, but I'm not sure that's enough."

"No, it's not enough, but I doubt anything will bother you. The creature expended a large amount of energy bullying me around last night, and it has probably retreated to its watery bed to regain its powers. You'll be safe, Anne," he said as I stepped over the room's threshold. "But, just in case, if anything happens, scream. Loudly."

He clicked the door closed behind me before I could utter another word.

Everything looked different in the pale morning light. I shook my head, asking myself if I truly believed all Lord Grey had said. My head fought against it. But I had experienced things I couldn't explain. I had seen and heard things that weren't there, and I'd been attacked by hands I couldn't touch, let alone remove. Whether I liked it or not, doubt was falling away, layer by layer.

As I placed my feet on the main hall's stone tiles, I traced their intricate designs with my eyes, so delicate, so subtle. I recalled how they had wriggled like worms under my hands.

"I mean you no harm," I whispered.

I passed the dining room, but retraced my steps and entered, turning toward the corner where the mirror hung suspended like a sheet of water. My hands tingled as I neared it, my eyes steady on my own reflection.

What lay coiled inside me that could make the glass strike out like a cornered animal? Where could it have come from? Not from my mother, or at least, not that I knew about, and certainly not from my father. But Lord Grey had also seemed to have no extending branch of magical ancestors. Perhaps he was right, it was just a talent handed out as randomly as blue eyes or red hair. In all honesty, I could have done without it. So far, all my wondrous power had done was antagonize inanimate objects, almost get me killed twice, and make a wraith long for my quick demise.

I sighed and left the dining room to slump off to my room. The silence in the manor was thick, and it had me listening for impending screams. I should be getting ready to work, not preparing to sleep. What would Ms. Simple say? And Dora; who knew the things she'd imagine! But they'd been the master's orders, and frankly, if God himself had come down and commanded me to work, I would have stuck my tongue out at him and gone to sleep.

I woke hours later to the golden rays of the afternoon sun resting on my bedclothes. A sense of panic filled me as I realized I'd slept most of the day away, all my chores forgotten. I dressed in a hurry and left my room.

"Well, look who's up," Dora said as she walked toward me from her room. She smiled, all teeth and gums, reminding me of a growling dog. "Lord Grey came down earlier to notify the rest of us lowly servants that we should allow you to sleep, since you had a long night. Mighty peculiar, if you ask me."

My cheeks warmed, but I kept my eyes on Dora's face. "We were talking. About," I swept my arm around, "all of this."

"Oh, I'm sure you were."

"I don't have to explain myself to you, Dora."

She chuckled. "No, of course not. Not when you have the master on your side."

"That's enough, Dora," Ms. Simple interrupted as she stepped out of her room. She looked tired, her eyes betraying her troubled mind. "Don't you think there's sufficient hostility in this house?"

Dora huffed and left the servant's quarters, anger trailing behind her.

"Don't pay her any mind, Anne. I'm afraid Dora is feeling the sting of jealousy."

"Jealousy? Over what?"

Ms. Simple smiled. "Regardless of what she says, she's always had a fondness for the young master, ever since she first met him, years ago. Even Miss Bellingham, God rest her soul, noticed Dora's infatuation the times she stayed at Rosewood. Of course, Lord Grey has never paid too much attention to it. On the contrary, the majority of the time, he does his best to avoid the poor girl. She can be rather frustrating, as I'm sure you've noticed." She took my hand in hers. "So, you see, Anne, for you to earn all this attention from Lord Grey must be a bitter tonic for Dora."

I nodded as her words swiped away the irritation I felt. "But, Ms. Simple, I didn't mean to hurt her like that." I paused as her words sunk in. "Wait, what happened to Miss Bellingham?"

"Oh, child, she died. Jumped to her death after her father's murder. A tragedy that marked poor Lord Grey almost as much as his mother's passing."

A flash of one of Lord Grey's memories glowed in my head. That letter he'd received, the one he'd torn to pieces, it had had a black ribbon around it. Only now did I recognize it as a mourning band.

"Speaking of Lord Grey," Ms. Simple said, "he has asked that you join him in the main hall. He's requested that we remain in our rooms while you work with him." She squeezed my hand. "Anne, what will you be working on?"

"I don't know, Ms. Simple. I honestly don't know."

As I walked out of the servant's quarters, I began to hear sounds form the main hall—the dull thuds of moving furniture. I moved through the hallways, afraid of the next disaster I might encounter, but as I rounded the corner, I saw Lord Grey, sleeves rolled up, trousers streaked with dust, dragging chairs from the nearby rooms.

I considered returning to bed. I was not up to whatever he was planning.

He turned and saw me. "Good, you're up."

"I'm sorry, sir, I did not realize I'd slept so long."

He was not listening to me, but eyeing the tiles under his feet, his brow creased in concentration.

"Sir, would you like me to prepare a meal for you? Sir?"

"What? Oh, no, I'm in no need of nourishment, but I suggest you eat something. You'll need it."

"But—"

He waved me in the vague direction of the kitchen, and I could do nothing but obey. The mess in the main hall didn't bode well. I had not an inkling what he needed chairs for, and I didn't want to ponder on it too long.

I didn't want to enter the kitchen, not after the previous night and the knowledge I now held, but as I couldn't very well step out for pastries at the corner shop, I mustered up my courage and entered. Taking a slice of bread quickly out of the pantry, I went into the hall to eat. The bread had the texture of sawdust. When I finished, I dragged myself back into Lord Grey's presence.

He was seated on the first stair-step, hands knitted together, his head resting on them.

"Sir."

His head sprang up and, for a moment, his kaleidoscope eyes did not know me. But as their swirling hues trailed my own, I saw the focus return to his face.

"Come here, Anne."

I moved next to him as he stood.

"I trust you ate something?"

"Yes, sir."

"Good."

Without warning, he pushed me onto one of the chairs, the one in the center of the hall. He didn't lay a finger on me, but struck me with a concrete wave of tentacled power. I yelped in painful surprise.

I only had time to stand before another muscular current flung me into another chair. I landed against the armrest, my back flaring in pain as fear filled my limbs. I gripped the chair and looked up at Lord Grey, who was as still and impassive as the staircase next to him—two dark nightmares.

I caught a flicker of movement in his eyes and knew he was about to attack again. In a reflex, I raised my arms and felt an uncoiling deep within me.

A weightlessness took over, as if I'd dropped all the flesh I possessed and became just my two eyes.

I could see Lord Grey through a circle of air that trembled, and his face was taut with effort. My concentration cracked as panic at what I was experiencing set in and the lead-like blood returned to my body, knocking me down into the chair. At least it was the same chair. He hadn't been able to move me.

I was trembling in shock. Even after all I'd seen the past three weeks, I was nowhere near used to facing evidence of that kind of power.

Lord Grey jogged toward me, pulling the first seat with him, and sat down in front of me with a sigh.

I flinched, but he raised his hands. "I'm not going to hurt you. I apologize that I had to frighten you, but I had to see what I could pull out of you. You see, with beginning students of magic, the powers only truly surface when the receptacle fears for his or her life. It's instinctual."

"That was a test?" My voice was harsh in my throat.

"Yes."

"Bloody wonderful. You nearly broke my back." I bit off the words. The nonsense had gone on long enough.

"I couldn't very well place you delicately on the chair, could I? Besides, I thought a chair would be better than the hard floor." He met my anger with sarcasm that only fueled my irritation.

I rose, ready to leave, but he took my arm in his hand. His fingers brushed my skin before he jerked them back in a quick recoil. As I watched, his body crumpled in a cough, making the anger I felt shift somewhat to concern. Since my skin still prickled where his flesh had met mine, and my back still ached from where I'd hit the chair, I wasn't in the most sympathetic of moods.

When he got his breathing under control, he spoke again. "I had to show you what you could do."

"And now what? What do you have in mind, sir?"

"Now, I have to teach you how to call up that power when and however you like. It needs to become an arm or a leg, just another dependable limb."

"And if I don't learn? What happens then?"

He stood. "You must leave or be killed."

"Those are my only options?"

He threw me a slicing stare. "They're better than mine."

There was nothing I could say to that; he was right.

"But the creature won't allow you to teach me, it'll do whatever it can to prevent it."

He nodded. "We must be smarter." His voice flattened. "Do you think you can manage that?"

"Yes, sir."

"Fetch me a candle, then."

With fear and confusion worming through my stomach, I ran to the kitchen and into the moldy pantry, where a whole box of candles rested. I grabbed one, then another just in case, and a box of matches.

In the hall, Lord Grey had pushed the chairs back and had cleared a space on the floor where he'd placed a simple candleholder. He stretched out his hand for the candle, taking caution not to touch me. He waved away the matches.

"All right, sit."

He curled his legs up, like an animal tucking in its tail, and sat on the cold stone tiles. The image of a manor's Lord, sitting cross-legged while attempting to force the candle to remain upright in its holder was a shock to my nerves. I coughed to veil a laugh.

"Damn thing . . ." he muttered.

"Here, sir, let me."

He flinched back as I took the wax candle in hand and squeezed forcefully into the tight, silver opening. It did not waver when I removed my hands.

As I looked up, I caught a fleeting smile on Lord Grey's lips. He cleared his throat.

"We'll begin with something simple, something we may repeat as much as necessary without tiring. I'm going to light this candle. It is your job to snuff it out. Do you understand?"

"Sir, I understand what you mean, but I don't know how I'll accomplish it."

He looked down at his hands, and brought one up along with his eyes. "This power we have is a muscle, like the muscles in our hands. As infants, our hands could not function with the delicacy they can now. What brought on that change? Use. Constant, dedicated use. And need, of course. If you can train your hands to sew, you can train your body to wield the energy it houses."

I winced. "Sewing is not my strongest ability."

"Wrong example, then. It makes no difference. The point remains: concentration and training are the keys."

He fell silent, his eyes on the naked candle. He inhaled, seeming to tug at the space around the wick and pulled a flame from the air.

I couldn't help gasping. He had created fire out of nothing! Lord Grey closed his eyes and then looked up at me. "Your turn."

I focused on the fire, its light still in the calm air. In silence, I commanded it to die, to flicker off in a trail of smoke. My mind was a labyrinth of words, crowding against each other to try to find the combination that would open the cache of power. Nothing was happening.

"Stop thinking," Lord Grey said, as if my thoughts were loud enough for him to hear.

"The flame is the only thing that matters, the only things that exists."

But my thoughts persisted, one chasing the other as I thought of all he'd told me the previous night. I shuddered and yanked my eyes away.

"Again," he said.

And so we did. Minutes turned into hours, the flame lowering as the wax fell in thick drops onto the silver. When my eyes blurred and my head's pounding was too painful to endure, I shook my head.

"Can't do it, sir."

"That's nonsense. You can, and you will."

He sighed and released all the tightness from his voice.

"That's probably enough for today, however. I'm afraid your brains will leak out of your ears." He leapt to his feet as I blinked back my shame. "We'll start fresh tomorrow. I don't know about you, but I could use some water."

"Yes, sir."

He headed toward the kitchen, while I picked the candle and myself up off the floor. I stared deeply into the flame, shook my head, and blew it out in one breath.

SEVENTEEN

THE SMELL OF CHARRED VEGETABLES WAS STRONG enough to be nauseating as I entered the kitchen. Lord Grey stood, facing out into the night as he drank water in long swallows.

Dora, or most likely Ms. Simple, had left me a covered dish at my place on the table, and I was sure the Master had one in the dining room also. I'd been hungry after the long hours in front of the candle, but the dish's smell alone made my face scrunch up.

Perhaps I could make a meal for the two of us, since Dora was probably sleeping and would not be able to take offense over something she knew nothing about.

Walking into the pantry, I peered at the items that were viable to use for dinner. Not much to choose from in terms of variety—potatoes, onions, more potatoes.

"I'm afraid there are not many food options left, sir."

He didn't turn. "John should be arriving any day now."

I rolled my eyes at his distraction. "Yes, sir. I just wanted you to be aware I won't be able to prepare an entirely satisfying meal."

"Oh, there's no need, at least, not for my sake." He turned and stepped across the floor to the doorway.

"Sir, you must eat something."

"Don't concern yourself with me." His words were harsh, but I would not be cowed. I could not have him half-starved in the madness we were submerged in.

"Sir. I will be bold enough to say you will not last long in the condition you are in. Too thin, too tired, and ill, I dare say. If something were to happen, we have little means of getting help. So, with all due respect, I will scramble up some dinner, and you will eat it."

I didn't look to see his reaction, but bent to pick up the lumpy potatoes and flaky onions, cradling them to my breast.

I didn't hear Lord Grey leave, but when I glanced about, he was gone. I set to concocting whatever culinary magic I could.

The best choice was a soup, potatoes and onions lending taste and texture to the otherwise pale broth. I gathered herbs, dried sprigs of rosemary that smelled like tree sap, ground pepper, and sweet basil that took command of the entire pot. I sipped a spoonful and, though a bit on the weak side, it had flavor and was at least burning hot. I took the time to toast some of the bread which was a day old, but still serviceable if crisped.

As I carried the serving tray with Lord Grey's meal to the dining room, my stomach began to wail again in hunger, a low lament that vibrated throughout my body.

To my surprise, Lord Grey was already seated in his chair, head in hand. He threw me a look that dripped irritation as I placed the tray before him. "There was a dish here for me already," he said.

I eyed the meal Dora had prepared and moved it aside. "It's better to have a fresh dish, not one that's been sitting there for hours." And would probably shrivel up his organs, I thought, but did not add.

He picked up his spoon, and I retreated.

"Where's your plate?" he asked.

"In the kitchen, sir."

"You couldn't manage to carry two plates?"

"Sir, why would I bring mine here just to return it to the kitchen?"

"Ah, so you're planning on eating there."

I stared. Was he daft? Need I run to the door and away from the lunatic and his rose-scented hallucinations?

"It's where I always eat, sir."

He sighed. "What nonsense. Bring your plate here, Anne. It's beyond ridiculous to have you across the house. There's more than enough room for the two of us."

"Sir!"

"It's ridiculous and dangerous. Bring your plate."

In confusion, a feeling that was becoming more familiar by the minute, I returned to the kitchen to fetch my plate.

I couldn't help noticing though, as I entered the dining room again, that Lord Grey had waited for me before beginning. Just good manners, I supposed.

He pointed to a chair on his right and I placed my food down. I stared straight ahead, but could still see as he lifted a spoonful of soup to his lips. He paused half-way through chewing some potato chunks, his eyes narrowing to dark slits.

"You know how to cook," he said.

"I was a scullery maid for many years, sir."

"A scullery maid." The chuckle woven through his voice made me shift to look at him.

"Is something amusing, sir?"

"Just the thought of it is quite funny. With your temper, I would never have let you near the knife drawer."

His eyes lifted from his plate in a surge of energy that sent my hands tingling. He held my eyes in his own for a few seconds, then placed his spoon down and cleared his throat.

I found I'd lost my appetite. My heart galloped at a painful speed, sending my blood racing in a frenzy through my veins. It felt peculiar to be sitting there, the two of us alone, sharing a meal as equals.

It was almost a relief when a cold current stepped like a person into the room. We both felt it, and exchanged a neutral glance, Lord Grey already encased behind his icy sarcasm once more.

I shivered as a wave of air passed behind me.

"It cannot harm you in this room, not with the mirror watching," Lord Grey said.

Small comfort when I felt like I was being swallowed up by winter.

The mirror began to hum with power, the symbols beneath its surface pulsing like a heart. Soon, the creature moved on to sit beside the master as he sipped his wine. I could see his knuckles through his thin skin, fury and pain gripping Lord Grey's slight body.

"That's enough," he said.

A low laugh bubbled out and the cold evaporated.

"I think we should attempt to get some sleep," he said, after we'd pushed the food around our plates for a few more minutes. His eyes closed in damp exhaustion. I nodded, then realized he couldn't see me.

"Yes, sir. All right."

Scrubbing our dishes clean took only a matter of minutes and soon, I was ready to sink into sleep. Even after the long slumber I'd had that morning, I felt heavy and sluggish. If anything, the nap had made me realize how tired I was. Like a sip of water when thirsty, I needed more.

As I was leaving the kitchen, I heard the painful sound of coughing trailing down the staircase. I moved toward it and listened. The sound jolted yet another memory loose. My mother, coughing through endless minutes at a time, her body shaking with the sharp spasms. Where were these memories coming from?

For long seconds, I waited for the intake of breath that would bring relief to Lord Grey's body.

I went back to the kitchen and put water to boil. My movements were automatic, my thoughts not interfering with what my body was doing. I rummaged through the pantry and found what I needed: a thick ginger root. I chopped it up, adding it to the pot of water and letting it simmer until it filled the kitchen with its sharp scent.

I poured the ginger water over tea leaves, and strained the concoction into a cup. I mixed in a strong dose of honey and stirred it all into a golden brew.

Tea cup and saucer in hand, I went back to the main hall and up the stairs. The second story was in complete darkness except for one sliver of light. Coughs punctuated my steps until I found myself before Lord Grey's door. I took a breath and knocked.

His face showed surprise as he opened the door, although he brought his features under control an instant later.

"Sir, I heard you coughing, and I thought tea would help ease the spasms. It has no magical properties that I know of, but it does provide some relief."

He took the cup from me and moved aside to allow me in. An image of Dora's face flashed in front of me. I hesitated.

"Come in, Anne. I won't bite, you know."

With a thin smile, I stepped into his antechamber again.

"Take a seat. And don't tell me 'no,'" he said, just as my mouth was opening. "What is it with you and chairs?"

I smiled and took the seat I'd used the previous night. Lord Grey sat down and took a sip of tea.

"Ginger," he said. "Interesting concoction."

"It is, sir. The woman who raised me always prepared it for me when I was ill."

"The woman who raised you?"

"Well, sir, my mother died when I was young, so the cook at Caldwell House took me in."

"I see." His voice was soft, his eyes locked on me. He had a slight flush to his skin.

"Sir, it looks as if you might have a fever."

"It's nothing, Anne. If you recall, I mentioned the demon feeds off my energy. It sometimes places a strain on my body."

I looked down at my hands. "Sir, I'm concerned about the name we need for the banishment. How will we ever learn it? The creature will never reveal it."

He sighed. "I have thought long on that, and I've come upon only one way. You will have to provoke it, Anne."

"I'm sorry, sir?"

"Wraiths toy with their prey, with what they are about to destroy. This one is no different. It won't be able to help itself from taunting you with the truth before attempting to take your life."

My face must have betrayed my shock.

"I would do it myself, but the creature would never tell me because it does not want to kill me. I could never provoke it enough." He clutched the tea cup tighter in his hands. "We wouldn't even consider attempting anything like that until you were ready to defend yourself, though. And you would not be alone. Do you understand, Anne?" His flushed face lifted to meet my eyes as he said softly, "I would be right there to help you. I wouldn't allow it to harm you."

I didn't know what to say to that. My mind reared back at putting my life in such danger. I couldn't turn myself into bait!

A stab went through my chest. But . . . but it could mean everyone in the manor would be free once again. Could I deny them that, after all they'd been through?

I could think of no other way of extracting the name we needed. I closed my eyes. "When, sir?"

"I don't know. When you're ready. When we're both ready."

I nodded and attempted to smile as my stomach churned with nerves. "Um, sir, I was also wondering why you asked me a few days ago if I was religious? Would it have helped defeat this creature?"

"No. On the contrary, it would have made it more difficult to bring your powers to the surface."

"Why, sir?"

"For one thing, that particular group of people doesn't take too kindly to magicians. I rather think you would have 'aided' me by burning me at the stake."

I did smile that time, despite my new worries.

Silence descended on us as he sipped his tea. At least his coughing had stopped.

As I watched the pain relax its hold on his face, I could picture him as he must have been before all of this had happened. Full of energy and laughter. Full of smiles for the people he loved . . . perhaps even for Miss Bellingham.

Suddenly, I began to feel uncomfortable.

"If you're done, sir, I'll take the cup back to the kitchen and let you rest."

"Yes, of course." He handed me the cup. "You should get some sleep also, Anne. We have more training to do tomorrow."

I nodded. "Goodnight, sir."

"Goodnight, Anne."

With a healthy dose of nerves in my veins, I marched back to my room, head held as high as I could manage without spraining anything.

As I was about to open my door, I heard another one opening behind me. I turned and saw Ms. Simple hovering on her room's threshold.

"Ms. Simple, are you all right?"

"I was going to ask you the same thing, Anne."

"Yes, I am." I gave her my most reassuring smile, even as Lord Grey's plan swirled in my head.

There was a moment of silence as she looked at me. "I knew there was something different about you when you arrived, and it seems I was right." She moved the few steps toward me. Her hair was down, released from her usual severe bun, and its length surprised me. The dim light played over the white streaks that snaked through it.

"Here," she said, holding out her right hand.

I took what she held: a small, silver cross.

"I don't know if it'll help any with what you and the master are doing, but I always feel safer when there's a cross nearby."

The metal was warm in my palm, warmed by Ms. Simple's hand. I smiled.

"Thank you. I've never had one of my own before."

A growl passed by me, low but resonant in the small hall. The cold had returned and with it, the fear.

"Go back to bed, Ms. Simple. It's safer."

She hesitated. Even in the shadows, I could see the bruises on her cheek, displaying the creature's hate.

"I'll be all right. It's best if we don't anger it." Not yet, at least.

She nodded and turned back to her room. The growling followed her until she closed the door behind her.

EIGHTEEN

I MADE SURE I WAS AWAKE BEFORE THE REST OF the household the following morning. Another day of Dora's sneering was more than I could handle with everything else that was occurring. As I entered the kitchen, I touched the cross, which I'd placed in my gown's pocket, and smiled. It might have been my imagination, but it still felt warm.

It wasn't long before I heard steps nearing, and I turned from scrubbing the kitchen table to see Dora enter, her eyes passing me by as if I were as invisible as the creature haunting us.

"Good morning, Dora."

She nodded vaguely in my direction.

"Dora, listen, I didn't mean to sound harsh yesterday. It's just been a difficult few weeks. Lord Grey thinks I can help him with this situation, that's why I have to spend time with him. That's all, honestly."

She paused slicing the bread that would be our breakfast. "So, you will be our savior. Anne the savior."

Bugger. "I didn't mean it to come out like that. Dora, could you please turn around? Please?"

With a sigh, she did. "What else do you want to 'explain' to me, Anne?"

"I know I'm new here and that you see me as some sort of threat to your position in the manor, even more now that I have contact with Lord Grey, but I wanted to be friends, Dora. We are all in this manor, facing whatever roams inside it, together."

"I don't care one bit if you spend time with the master, but just know that whatever it is you're thinking will happen with him—"

"But I'm not—"

"Don't interrupt! Whatever you think could happen between the two of you, won't. He *loves* her, Miss Bellingham. He always has. He could never care for a servant."

Her words shook me, the anger behind them chilling me more than anything the wraith could fashion. I could not find my voice.

She continued. "You know, if it weren't for you, nothing would have gotten as terrible as it has. I've realized that. You are the cause of all these horrid things. Of getting the cook attacked badly enough to make her lose an eye. She was my aunt, you know, and now, no one will hire her. She's practically destitute."

"I'm sorry, Dora. I wasn't aware of that."

"No, of course you weren't. You're as innocent as a lamb, and yet, you've angered this creature. You've put us all in danger."

As if to accent her words, there was a hiss of air that flew by me, strong enough to push Dora back against the sink. She gasped as the knife she'd been wielding was thrown across the room to clatter on the stone floor.

Dora looked at me. "Am I supposed to be thankful you're here, Anne, when this is what it means?"

She was right. "No, Dora, you're not."

After that rather rough beginning to the morning, I wasn't in the most forgiving mood to deal with the candle in front of me.

There was no luck in that section either. No matter how hard I tried, how much I concentrated, the flame was still glowing with a stubbornness that was unseemly. Lord Grey was becoming as frustrated as I was, I could tell.

"I'd rather thought you would have gotten this by now, Anne."

"I'm sorry, sir."

"Well, your powers have been dormant for far too long. I should have taken that into account. Let's try something else."

Although I nodded, I could have thought of about a thousand other things I'd prefer to do, including sewing.

He stood and I followed him.

"Now, when we get ready to do what we have to do to destroy this creature, you will need to speak a certain few magic words. A chant, if you will."

"But sir, you didn't need a chant that first time with the Brothers."

"True, but that was a wild creature. This one we face now requires the additional power that these particular words bring. I assume you've never done such a thing as chanting before?"

"No, sir."

"I will teach you, then, how to properly use your voice in magic. First, you must understand that all the words we speak have power behind them, even commonplace words. Your name, for example, defines part of who you are. As you are now well aware, for someone to know your name is a powerful thing, to be used for good or ill. For chanting, all that is required is for you to know, to understand, that the words you speak are weapons as powerful as a dagger or a pistol, and then to add a little air beneath them. Watch."

He stood still, opened his mouth and spoke a word that meant nothing to me. I assumed it was one of the magical ones he'd spoken about.

"What did you feel?" he asked.

"Nothing, sir, I'm sorry."

"Stop apologizing, Anne. You weren't supposed to feel anything because I put no strength behind the word. Now, hear this."

He repeated the word. It was just as quiet as the first time, and yet his voice echoed in the hall, vibrating against my very skin.

"Did you feel the difference?"

"Yes, sir, but how did you do it?"

He walked toward me, standing so close I could feel his warmth pushing against me. He raised one hand and brought it up to my chest, a little above where my rib bones ended. He didn't touch me, but I felt his hand nonetheless.

"You speak the word from there. From your center. That's where your power comes from. In the chant you will use, there is a word 'athana,' which means 'help.' I want you to practice with that one."

He stepped back and allowed me more room. The word filled my mouth as I breathed, contemplating what Lord Grey had just told me.

"Athana," I said.

He shook his head. "Try again. Concentrate."

I thought of the way he'd said it, a caress of syllables. I felt the warmth of his hand in my very center, my heartbeat meeting it in an orb of energy. "Athana."

My voice leapt out of my body like water from a fountain and hovered in mid-air. I blinked in surprise.

"Very nice, Anne. At least you have that figured out. Now, back to the candle."

By the time I found myself in the kitchen for supper, I'd had just about enough of candles and Lords, and only wanted my bed to materialize in front of me. Ms. Simple poured more food on my plate with a murmur of keeping my strength up, but I could have fallen asleep right there, my head in the stew.

I did notice, though, that Mr. Keery was not present.

"He's been feeling a bit ill," Dora said, the only words she addressed to me the entire evening.

"We've taken him a dish to the stables, so that he can remain in bed."

If I'd been less tired, perhaps I would have felt the warning in the air. But I didn't. I just finished my duties and plunged into bed. I did not even bother taking my shoes off. A blessing, that.

I groaned as the sound woke me. Really, this was too much. As I rose to full consciousness, I realized it was not the usual scratching at my door I was hearing, but a loud pounding.

"Anne! Anne!"

Leaping off the bed, I rushed to the bolted door while my heart beat out a warning. Dora's face pierced through the darkness, as white as her gown, her eyes raw with crying.

"I don't know what to do, Anne! Help me!" Her hands grabbed at me, yanking me into the hallway.

"What's the matter? Dora, what's wrong?"

"Ms. Simple, Mr. Keery."

"What? What about them? Dora!"

I chased after her as she sprinted off to the kitchen. Voices leapt up like flames: Ms. Simple's taut and thin, and another, that *other* one—the wraith's voice. I slammed into Dora's back as she froze in front of the kitchen door.

"And what exactly do you plan to do, Ms. Simple? Simple, mimple, wimple. Huh? What does your little brain tell you to do?"

I flinched as I realized the voice coming out of Mr. Keery's throat was not his own. It was not the usual quiet murmur, but the cold chuckling that had been trailing us.

"Mr. Keery, please." Ms. Simple moved to the left, revealing the scene's full madness. Mr. Keery, soaked and covered in hay, brandishing a make-shift torch. A bitter smell reached my nose and I knew he was not dripping water, but oil, the drops crashing to the floor with each twitch of his body.

"Mr. Keery, Peter, please. Give me the torch." Ms. Simple's shaking hands extended, but a low growl and a strike forward from the coachman pushed her away.

"Peter."

"Peter Peter Peter Peter Peter." The voice rose in a slithering cackle, upwards until it cracked into a laugh. "You still think this is Peter Keery. Idiotic woman."

I shook off the paralysis that bound me and stepped into the swaying light from the torch. The coachman's eyes rotated to me. His smile widened.

"You're just who I wanted to see, pretty Anne." He limped to me, one of his ankles twisted into a grotesque split of skin and bone. My first thought was to run backward, away from the creature's presence, but I grit my teeth against the fear and held my ground.

A wave of fragrant air brushed my back and a high voice spoke from over my shoulder.

"That's enough," Lord Grey said.

"You think so, August? Hmm? It's not been nearly enough." Mr. Keery's body swayed. "I see you are getting closer to this pretty lass. She's going to help you unravel a few 'issues.'" He barked a laugh.

My cheeks burned at the insinuations, but I felt Lord Grey's hands grasp my arms firmly, moving me sideways and away from the coach-man's eyes.

"She's just a maid, and you know it." Lord Grey's profile was sharp against the night.

"Oh ho, no. I don't think that's all she is. Much more than that, August, you silly boy."

Lord Grey lifted one hand and spoke a couplet of words under his breath.

Mr. Keery smiled. "I think it's time to be rid of the rest of the cast, don't you, Anne? Let's make it a little cozier for the three of us."

In a second, the flames had trailed up the coachman's arms, up to his head and down to his legs. A scream like breaking glass filled the kitchen, and the voice spoke again from above us.

"I'll be seeing you, sweet girl."

Dora began to whimper behind me, a swallowed squeal trapped inside her body, while Ms. Simple pressed herself flat against the farthest wall.

"Anne!" One look from Lord Grey was all it took to break my paralysis and set me running to the main hall. I yanked the first curtain I came upon, pulling its heavy weight down, pole and all, and ripped the fabric off. I ran back to the kitchen trailing dark cloth.

Lord Grey grasped one end and together we smothered Mr. Keery's body, throwing him to the floor as his screams dug into our heads.

"We need to turn him!" I screamed at Lord Grey, who nodded and did as I said.

All sound except for our shifting clothes stopped. When I could see no smoke or fire trailing out of the curtain, I relaxed my grip.

"Is he alive, sir?" I asked.

"I don't know." He pulled back a corner of fabric, revealing peels of black skin and bubbling flesh that gurgled with every breath. Oh, thank God, he was breathing.

I had seen my share of burns working in a fully-functioning, hectic kitchen, but nothing could have prepared me for the pulsing boil Mr. Keery had become.

"Sir, we need to get him to a doctor."

Lord Grey looked at me, a flash of fear smothered by reason. "Of course."

Ms. Simple stepped toward us. "We need to get out of here. We need to leave. I won't stay another moment in this cursed place." Her voice shook with fear and anger. "Dora, come on. I've had enough. We're leaving."

"But you won't be allowed! The wraith will stop you."

Lord Grey shook his head. "Didn't you hear it? It gave its permission. It wants the two of us alone with it, Anne, but you must attempt to leave with them." He sighed. "Please, take Peter with you and find him a doctor. I can't do it myself."

His voice was soft, without inflection.

"Fine, but we're going, now." Ms. Simple pulled on Dora to get her to stop crying. "Anne, come on."

I knew I should go. I could picture my father's horrified expression just for entertaining the notion of staying unsupervised with the Lord of the house. And leaving was the only logical thing to do when your life has been threatened for days without pause, but as Lord Grey's eyes searched mine, I saw that stain of fear. He couldn't leave. He was sick and needed help, and like it or not, I was the only one who could provide it.

"No, I'll stay," I said, pushing my father's shocked voice backward for the first time in my life.

The young man in front of me flinched.

"That's precisely what the wraith wants, to have you here in its domain where it can harm you."

"Nevertheless, I will stay."

Ms. Simple gasped. "No, Anne, come with us! You'll die here!"

"I can't. I'm sorry. I can help end all of this, forever."

Ms. Simple wrapped her arms around me, her hands clasping me tightly. With grim amusement, I realized it was the second time in a few months I'd had to separate myself from someone who cared about me. I prayed it'd be the last.

As she left the kitchen with Dora, I stood.

"I'll see to the horses."

NINETEEN

BETWEEN ALL OF US, WE MANAGED TO GET
Mr. Keery's collapsing body into the coach. I arranged pillows and blankets
all around him. The poor man could only moan, an animal sound that was
weak, but that at least announced he still clutched to life.

Dora had stopped whimpering, but she seemed hollow, her
thoughts roaming somewhere else while her body got her bags stowed
in the carriage. She would be traveling inside, next to Mr. Keery. Lord
Grey was as silent as the rest of us. He was unreadable, nothing swept
through his eyes, at least, nothing I could recognize.

"Ms. Simple, can you manage?" he finally asked as he placed a large
purse in her trembling hands.

She nodded once and tucked the purse into her traveling cloak.

"As soon as you reach the nearby manor, have one of their men
drive you to London. I hate to send you out alone."

"We can manage." Without another word, Ms. Simple seated
herself in the driver's seat and jerked the bleary-eyed horses into
movement.

"Goodbye, Ms. Simple, Dora," I said.

Lord Grey waited to see them cross the border and ride away from the manor. He sighed with relief as they disappeared, swallowed by the trees. He looked at me, then walked toward the house shrouded in darkness, his steps deflating the soft snow.

I had to be out of my mind. I'd been concerned about entering the master's rooms without a chaperone and now, here I was, volunteering to stay all alone with him, for who knew how long. I doubted the two frightened women would return anytime soon.

All the continuous activity had swept the past hour from my head, but it all began to return to the forefront. What would happen to Mr. Keery? Would he live?

Sleep was not an option at the moment, and Lord Grey seemed to realize it, since he was already in the kitchen, attempting to clean up the remnants of the night's horror. I brought out rags and the vinegar, ready to scrub the smell of smoke from the floor.

"Is the nearest manor close, sir?"

"No." His hands shook as he picked up large pieces of glass from a smashed lamp. "We are so far away from everything. You should have left, Anne," he whispered. "This is not going to get any better."

I stepped closer to him, feeling that peculiar warmth of his energy pulling on mine. "We'll be all right, sir. You'll see."

He turned and smiled sadly. Feeling a strange flutter in my stomach, I cleared my throat and got back to work.

Neither of us felt much like training; we were too tired, still too stunned to concentrate. After a pathetic effort on my part to repeat the exercise from the previous day, Lord Grey released me.

"There's no point in attempting anything today. Even I feel depleted of all magical energy. I can't expect you to be more focused."

He nodded my release and retreated to the dining room with a book. As for me, I knew just what I needed to do to take my mind off of everything: I'd scrub the house clean, once and for all.

When every muscle ached, and my mind was buoyed by a cloud of dust, I stopped and walked to the dining room, now as spotless as it had ever been. I'd had to ask Lord Grey for help with the mirror, since it did not feel any friendlier toward me, but at least, it was now resplendent on the wall. Lord Grey had sneezed with the dust until I thought he'd faint, but it had brightened the mood a bit, the noise making us feel less lonely in the large manor. We were both beginning to feel more like ourselves.

We ate together in the dining room and spoke only a few words as we battled with the sleep that was catching up with us.

"I think I need to retire, Anne. I'm about to collapse as I sit."

"Of course, sir."

He was already up and walking out of the room. I sighed and picked up our plates. I debated whether to leave the dishes for the morning, but my years of training would not be silenced. I couldn't leave a dish unwashed.

But by the time I finished, a few minutes later, fright was competing with exhaustion. As I walked toward my room, I began to feel the cold again, resonating at its highest pitch, a crystal-shattering tone that seemed to crush me with its weight. I covered my face with my hands. I didn't know what to do as I stood there in the dark hallway, my eyes sewn together against whatever horror lay unseen beyond them.

"I can't," I whispered.

Refusing to open my eyes, I turned and walked back toward the dining room. I would rather sleep in there, under the gaze of the mirror, even if I had to sleep in a chair, than lay down in the pit that was my room.

As I was about to enter, I heard footsteps on the staircase, real enough to know it was not a spectral being, but Lord Grey.

"I just realized I'd left you to be murdered in your bed, so I figured I'd come down and see if you still breathed." The master's voice echoed against the stones.

I grimaced. "As you can see, sir, I'm still living. But, yes, I was also a tad concerned as to where I would be safest."

"And where has your brain guided you, Anne?"

I pointed to the door on my left.

"I was planning on sleeping in there."

"What, in a chair?"

"Yes, sir."

"Your brain is not to be trusted, then. Utter nonsense."

I leashed my irritation and answered with as much patience as I could muster. It had been a long day and his changes in mood were wearing me out. "Where do you suggest I sleep, sir?"

"Follow me."

I traipsed after him (yet again), as he climbed the stairs, his hands never touching the banister, while mine squeezed it until my joints ached.

He led me toward his chambers and made a right turn, bringing us to a room that shared a wall with his own.

"This was my mother's personal study. It hasn't been aired in a while, but it has a somewhat comfortable settee."

He opened the door, revealing a room a bit larger than mine, with a delicate desk, chair and bookcase standing against the walls like wooden guards. The wallpaper was of the lightest blue, more like the color found in a nursery room, than in a Lady's.

"It used to be my room, as an infant," Lord Gray said, as if he'd read my thoughts. I had the briefest flash of a dark-haired boy staring up at those blue walls, dreaming of the ocean or of an endless sky. I shook my head.

"It's charming," I said.

"If anything disturbs you, I will be able to hear and come to your assistance in a matter of seconds. I will place a protective chant over the door, which won't help all that much, but which will, at least, give me some time. Bolt the door behind me, of course."

"There's nothing else I can do to protect myself?" I asked.

He shrugged and curled a lip. "Have prayers ever done anything for you?"

I shook my head.

"Then, that's all I can tell you."

He turned around and walked out of the room, closing the door behind him.

"Remember," he said, from the other side of the door, "if anything tries to slaughter you, scream."

A high chant trembled against the wood, a caressing of consonants in Lord Grey's sharp voice. A shiver shook me as I listened, and my eyes closed. The chant was long and knotted, and I began to feel its cadence seeping into my very bones, the words brushing me, until silence released me. I heard Lord Grey's door closing behind him.

With a sigh I crossed to the lumpy settee and sat down, prepared for anything.

TWENTY

IT WAS A PLEASANT SURPRISE, THEREFORE, WHEN only the sounds of scratches managed to pierce the silence. It was incredible how quickly the body and the mind adjusted to just about everything. I sighed as the sound woke me, but the fear that had shaken me the previous few nights was a tiny thing inside me. I lay in the stiff settee and listened as the creature wore itself out.

While I courted sleep, I wondered why the wraith was so bent on causing Lord Grey harm. Why didn't it recognize him as its master? There had to be something we were missing. I thought about the up-coming struggle we would have with it, and I flinched. But I'd worry about it when it was time, not now. As it was, I was nowhere close enough to being ready.

When, minutes later, the creature finally gave up, I released my thoughts and sank once more into sleep.

Hours later, I woke to a quiet house. I rose and stretched the tightness out of my muscles. Stepping up to a round mirror that hung on one of the walls, I saw that I looked much more rested than I had since arriving at Rosewood Manor. My eyes were alert, no purple marks pulling at the surrounding skin, even after the previous night's terror. I pinned my waves of curls into a serviceable bun.

I slid out of the room, past Lord Grey's silent door and down the stairs. Ms. Simple and Dora should have made it to whatever help was available already. Maybe Mr. Keery was out of danger. My thoughts wavered. Maybe he was already dead. I pushed the thought away and focused on the things I could do something about.

It was much cooler downstairs and I shivered as I moved toward the kitchen to see what I could manage for breakfast. I hoped the delivery man would arrive soon, otherwise, the two of us would be eating potato soup for the next few meals.

I boiled coffee and toasted the last bits of petrified bread, slathering preserves on my slice to grant it a bit of sweetness in an effort to neutralize the bitter, burnt flavor.

Not knowing what time Lord Grey would wake, I left a covered plate and saucer on the dining table and proceeded to do a bit of cleaning. The house didn't really need it, as I'd just scrubbed it raw the day before, but I had nothing else to do.

I started with the staircase, erasing my fingerprints from the previous night, oiling the wood until it shone, reflecting the morning sunlight on its surface. Not being able to help myself, I smiled. A job well done.

I was halfway through scrubbing the parlor floor again when I heard footsteps descending. The steps drew near.

"Already up and about, huh?" Lord Grey spoke from the doorway.

"Yes, sir, just doing some chores."

"I see."

"There is some breakfast waiting in the dining room, if you'd care to eat something, sir."

"Will you yell at me if I don't?" His voice was a light, fluttering thing.

"No, sir. Of course not."

He hovered as I continued scrubbing. "I would like to continue with your training, Anne."

I stopped moving, but didn't turn around. "As you wish, sir."

I followed him back out into the main hall, my enthusiasm not quite matching his own. In all honesty, I doubted I would make much progress, but I fetched the candle and its holder and placed them back on the floor. We sat down.

Lord Grey pulled the flame out again, right from the air, and looked up.

"All right, Anne, let's flex that muscle of yours."

Sighing, I let my eyes fall on the fire, my insides already gurgling in frustration. I tried. I truly did. My eyes grew dry and itchy as the minutes passed and the flame still glowed in mockery. I let my head fall into my hands.

"Sir, I can't do it. I don't know how."

His next words shocked me. "Remove your shoes."

"Sir?"

"Remove your shoes, Anne."

It was not proper; my father would have a coronary if he found out. The voice in my head, sounding more like myself than I'd ever heard it, bit out at me: *your father is not here.*

I uncoiled my legs and pulled my shoes off, revealing socks worn and thin.

"Your socks too," he said.

I didn't allow myself to question, but bared my feet in an instant. Their paleness glowed on the stone floors, making me weak with an embarrassment I tried to conceal from the sure young man before me.

Lord Grey stood and moved behind me, kneeling back down in a graceful, silent wave of warm energy. "Unpin your hair."

I reached up, feeling his eyes on my hands as I freed my curls in a tumble of brown sighs.

His voice brushed against me. "I want you to understand, to *feel* yourself in control. To look beyond the rules, the 'shouldn'ts,' the boundaries of our world. All that matters is that flame. Feel the cold stone under your feet, your hair's weight on your shoulders, everything that makes you who you are, Anne. Everything that gives you dominion over that flame."

I could feel his body's warmth pulsing against my back, only a gap of air separating our different energies. I closed my eyes and allowed my head to fall back, letting my hair cascade down.

At first, nothing happened. But as I concentrated on the energy beside me, so close, so strong, my hands began to tingle. I allowed them to open and released their power. Dizziness overtook me, a quick shake of weightlessness that soon evaporated.

"Open your eyes," Lord Grey whispered into my ear.

I did. The flame had disappeared.

The rest of the afternoon was spent in endless repetition, until the fire was carved into my very pupils. But Lord Grey was right, the more I practiced, the easier it became, until it only took a few seconds to snuff the dwindling candle out.

He sat before me, cradling a book on his knees, only lifting his eyes to relight the fire when needed.

As the sun dipped down and the light became opaque against the stones, Lord Grey slammed the book down and stood.

"I think that's enough. You seem to have mastered it, and it's about time."

I attempted to stand, but my body was stiff, as if I'd been nailed to the floor, my muscles fused together to create one huge, painful lump of flesh.

"Ouch," I said.

Lord Grey neared. "I'd help you up if I could, but unless you'd like another burn, I think it best if I keep my hands to myself."

"Of course, sir." With a grunt and a curse that was accompanied by the master's dry laughter, I stood.

"Tomorrow, we'll begin something harder, Anne. More like the first test with the chairs. We don't have the luxury of taking the lessons at our leisure."

As if summoned by his words, a current of frozen air passed by us, encircling us.

"August, are you enjoying your little whore?" the voice spat out.

Even Lord Grey flinched at the word dripping with anger, but he recovered before I did.

"I was wondering when you'd show up."

"Were you now, little August?"

A current pushed into Lord Grey's back, moving him forward, making him lose his balance. I moved to help him, but he managed to steady himself, his face bathed in the afternoon sunlight. A chant rose from his lips like a silver chain, consonants clanking all around the room. My skin prickled with the sudden energy, my ears popping as my whole body fought against the onslaught. I felt the tipping point, the spilling over of Lord Grey's powers, coating every surface around us.

The wraith was silent for a heartbeat, then, in a whirl of invisible blades, it flung itself at Lord Grey's body with a roar as thick as a lion's.

Screams took over the hall—anguished cries of pain and triumphant shrieks that clashed with each other. In an instant, I was in the middle of it all, my back being pummeled by the wraith's fury as I attempted to separate the two engulfing powers. I rounded on the attacking creature. I couldn't see it, but I could feel it as it circled us.

"Get out!" I screamed.

"That's not polite, Anne."

"Out! Or I'll—"

"You'll what? All I've seen you do is blow out a candle. What could you possibly do to me?" With that, it slapped me, hard, a freezing bruise already staining my cheek. My hands began to warm, but before I had the chance to see what I could do, the cold was gone. The creature had fled.

I turned around. Lord Grey was leaning against a wall, deep cuts having torn at his clothes and the skin underneath them until blood pooled in puddles at his feet.

"Sir!" I ran up to him, but he put his hand up.

"Please don't touch me, Anne."

I took stock of his injuries—most were superficial, large paper cuts, but one of them concerned me. His wrist was a well of blood.

"Sir, I need you to sit. Hold your wrist with your other hand. Press it down."

When he obeyed, I ran to the kitchen and pulled out the first table-cloth I came upon. Taking a knife to one frilled corner, I yanked down, ripping a long white strip of linen.

What would I do if he needed medical attention? There were no horses left, and the nearest manor was a half day away, longer in the snow. I pushed the thoughts out of my head and ran back to kneel beside Lord Grey's pale, drooping form.

His trousers were drenched in blood, and his eyes fluttered as every heartbeat sent more and more of his life-force onto the floor.

With irrational anger, I remembered he hadn't had any sustenance since the previous night.

"Sir! Sir! Wake up. I'm going to wrap this around your wrist."

"No . . . I'll do it."

"No, you can't bloody well do it!" I snarled and pulled his hand away from the wound. A shock of fire burned me, but I grit my teeth and grasped his slashed wrist. Ignoring the scorching that was overwhelming my hands and the painful moans I was drawing from him, I wrapped the linen as tight as I could around his wrist until the blood disappeared beneath the white cloth.

I didn't know if that would keep him from bleeding out. I had no knowledge of doctoring aside from the more common household injuries. He had winced when I'd first touched him, but now, Lord Grey was still. Unconscious, most likely. I looked down at my hands, which were stained with blood. My own or his? No way to tell. A sob ripped through me as nerves abandoned my system, leaving only a sense of despair so black it seemed to swallow me whole.

What seemed like hours later, I took my emotion's reins back and rose on legs that trembled.

Lord Grey was slumped against the wall, fully owning up to his name. His breathing, however, was steadier, and the blood appeared to have stopped dripping out. Through the ripped clothing, his ribs peered out, the thin layer of skin stretching like a stocking every time he inhaled. The skin there was even paler, as powdery white as the dust that permeated most of the furniture.

No wonder he'd collapsed after so much blood loss. It was a surprise he hadn't died.

Walking once again to the kitchen, I looked for anything that would give his body what it needed to recover. There were no smelling salts in the manor, I knew that, but vinegar would do the trick. I looked around for anything to strengthen his blood, perhaps something sweet, to force down the master's throat. I considered wine, but decided against its dizzying abilities. It would most likely do more harm to his depleted system.

I decided jam would have to do. Gripping a spoon, the vinegar bottle, and a jar of strawberry jam, I flung myself back into the corridor and headed to the main hall.

He hadn't moved at all. I uncorked the vinegar bottle, its scent reaching up, and placed it right beneath Lord Grey's nose. His next inhale brought his eyelids back up. His strange eyes, a deep gold, like honey in shadows, steadied on mine, and his curling lip reassured me.

"There's no need to look at me like that. I'm not dying." His voice was muted and harsh.

"You almost did, sir."

He looked down at his swaddled wrist and the smile flew away. "Ah. Just a fainting spell."

"Here." I brought a brimming spoonful of preserves close to his face. "Have some. It's the only sugar I could find in the house, unless you'd like to chew sugar cubes like a horse."

"I'm fine."

"You are not fine, and you will eat this, or I'm walking out that door, sir." I gestured with the hand that still held the spoon, naturally splattering chunks of strawberry everywhere.

Lord Grey closed his eyes and wheezed out a laugh. "All right, but I will not be fed like an infant." He stretched out his uninjured hand and dipped the spoon back into the jar, bringing it up full, and into his mouth.

He shook his head and shivered. "That's a substantial amount of sugar."

"Yes, and your blood needs it. Have another, sir."

He obeyed.

"How did you know to do this?" He raised his bandaged arm.

"Seemed like the logical thing to do. Otherwise, the entire floor would have been soaked in your blood."

"And we can't have that. Too much cleaning." His voice sharpened with sarcasm.

"Sir, that is not what I meant."

Grunting, he pressed his back against the wall for support and attempted to stand. He wobbled on his feet.

When I saw his face lose whatever hints of color it had gained, I leapt up, just in time to catch him as he slumped forward. Fire burned against every point where our skins met.

"Damn it, sir, you're not ready to be standing."

He shook his head, clinging to consciousness, the pain we both felt helping him hold on. The smell of roses mingled with the silver scent of blood, making my head spin as he rested against me. I had to bite my lip to keep from screaming at the electric current that kept jolting me. We needed to move to somewhere I could lay him down, and quickly.

"Sir, grab on to my shoulder, put your weight on me."

"But the burns . . ."

"Yes, it's quite awful, so the sooner we get to a chair or something, the better."

"The dining room."

"All right, sir."

I whimpered as I lifted his arm around my shoulders, allowing me to slip into the crook, and bracing his weight. His scant body was easy to maneuver into the dining room. I eased him onto a chair, my skin separating from his, and pulled another chair in front of him to hold his legs.

"One moment, sir." I left the room and entered the parlor, where I gathered some of the softer sofa pillows. I returned to Lord Grey and placed them behind his back to grant him as much comfort as the situation allowed. He would have been better off in bed, but until he regained his strength, the dining room chairs would have to be enough. Last thing I wanted was another near tumble down the stairs.

A bit of color seemed to have returned to his cheeks as I hovered by the table, my hands finding no rest in their nervousness.

"Will you sit, Anne? You're making my skin crawl."

I obeyed, although, I had no idea how I would sit still.

"Quick thinking there, Anne. I imagine I would be dead, or very near it, if it weren't for you."

"It was nothing, sir."

"Just your duty, I suppose."

My cheeks warmed. "That's right, sir."

He laughed. "I'm sure you curse the day you stepped foot in this manor."

The dampened tone to his voice alarmed me. I peered into his face. It was as closed as always.

I opened my mouth, but he raised a trembling hand, the skin dry as plaster.

"Don't lie."

I swallowed. "Well, sir, it's been a difficult few weeks. It was not what I expected."

"I can imagine not." He looked at me, then down at his raw hands. "You said you worked as a scullery maid?"

"When I was very young, sir. I entered Lady Caldwell's service when I was almost seven."

"My goodness!" The shock enlivened his face.

"It's not unusual, sir, to enter service that young, especially when your mother works in the same household."

"As yours did?"

"Yes, sir. She was Lady Caldwell's personal maid."

"Tell me about your mother."

"There's not much to tell, sir. I hardly remember her—she died almost immediately after I entered Caldwell House. Of consumption."

"Ah."

"She was a wonderful servant."

"I'm sure there was more to her than that."

I lowered my gaze as I tried to bring the imprint of the woman who bore me up to my eyes. It was not as difficult as it had always been. She felt closer to me now, a real person, not a phantom memory.

"She had the most wonderful smell, the crisp white of starch, and a sweet undertone from the creams she wore for her dry skin. Too many years of washing dishes. Mary always told me I was a lot like her. She had so much energy. She was willing to feel every emotion. But . . ." I paused. The memories that had been making themselves known through the last few weeks joined together with Mary's words. I was suddenly aware of knowledge I'd pushed aside, but which now rang through me like a bell's chime.

"What, Anne?"

I took a shaky breath. "She wasn't brave. She disliked her life, even her marriage, yet she did nothing to change them. For herself, or for me. She could have, if she'd truly wanted to." I shook my head. "She wasn't brave enough." Tears crowded my eyes.

Lord Grey watched me, the expression on his pale face indecipherable in the late afternoon light. "Then you are nothing like her, Anne."

I brushed my eyes and tried to smile, but my lips quivered. I wasn't so sure.

Lord Grey cleared his throat. "What of your father, is he still alive?"

"Yes, thankfully. He's Lord Exter's manservant. I don't see him much, but it is still a comfort to know he is somewhere in the world."

"Yes, I imagine it is."

I bit my lip at his subdued tone. I hadn't meant to remind him of his own solitude.

"And siblings, Anne?"

"Well, sir, I was raised alongside Elsie, another maid at Caldwell House. She is my sister in everything but blood. We'd never been apart before I took this position."

His face darkened. "I shouldn't have separated you from her, then."

"You didn't know, sir."

Sighing, he leant back against the pillows.

"It's been a horrid few weeks, I know," he said. "Anne, I'm not holding you prisoner. I was pondering this today, and maybe you misunderstood me. We still can't attempt to cast the wraith out, and I don't know when we will be ready. It could be weeks of this nightmare. You are free to leave if all of this becomes too much of a weight. You must realize by now, that your life is roaming in a dangerous domain by staying here."

"Sir, I could not leave you on your own."

He stiffened. "I can manage."

"Like you 'managed' today?" The words slid out before I could trim them with propriety.

He chuckled and shook his head. I lowered my eyes to my hands to keep the embarrassment I felt as hidden as possible, but when I raised them once more, I found Lord Grey's face poised on a very different expression than I'd ever seen. A look of warmth, of almost tenderness, softened his stone-like features.

My heart sped up without my permission, a precognitive contraction that I would forever recall.

"I don't know if you realize just what you're capable of," he said. "Not only do you have a rare ability that could help me end all of this, but you have the rarer skill of making me laugh. I know that doesn't mean anything to you," he said as I opened my mouth, "but to me, it is a breath of the freshest air."

The memory of Dora's words froze the smile I was about to give Lord Grey. And Miss Bellingham, what of her?

The pounding in my chest increased, sending my skin tingling in a strange way that had nothing to do with my abilities, and everything to do with the confusion the man before me created.

TWENTY-ONE

I MANAGED, GOD KNOWS HOW, TO KEEP LORD Grey resting the entire following day. It was hard going, with his seeming inability to keep still for more than a few minutes, but I stood guard by his door. I practiced, through the long hours, with the candle, lighting it in a very non-magical way, and snuffing it out with my coil of power. It was becoming easier.

Around midday, I climbed down the stairs to the kitchen to prepare whatever I could find for lunch. If there was nothing more substantial than jam, then that's what we'd eat. Thankfully, I did not have to resort to such barbaric measures, since I found a tin of digestive biscuits which looked pretty much intact. No wonder, really, since they were about as tasteful as paper. To make up for that, I prepared Lord Grey's ginger tea, mixing it as strong as I could without it tasting like liquid fire.

Armed with the tin, the jam and the tea, I traipsed yet again up to Lord Grey's door. The manor's air felt lighter this morning, even calm, making it seem like the previous afternoon's violence had not occurred. I knew better, of course, but still, it was nice to feel a bit of tranquility.

Lord Grey was sitting up in his sofa. He'd refused to lie in bed. His hair was tousled, and he looked rather charming in his robe, the blanket

I'd thrown over him a twisted mess. My heart seemed to hitch a bit, making my hands shakier than was wise when holding a tray of china.

"How are you feeling, sir?"

"I'm fine, Anne. Really. It's ludicrous for me to be lying like an invalid because of a cut."

I'd found that the best way of dealing with his logic when it came to health was to ignore him, which is what I did, busying myself with the biscuits and the plates.

"What in God's name is that?" He peered at the disk crowned with jam I passed him.

"The only thing I could find, sir." I bit into mine and almost chipped a tooth. Hmm. I'd better wait for the jam to soften it up a tad.

When I glanced up, Lord Grey was staring at me, a slight smile on his face. I felt my cheeks redden under his eyes. I took another bite.

"Anne, I'm surprised," he said.

"Why, sir?"

"You're actually sitting."

I looked down to find myself comfortable in one of his chairs. I smiled, my heart speeding up once again.

When, hours later, Lord Grey stood and declared he wanted a quick walk around the grounds, I didn't stop him. I needed to get away from him, to clear my head and bail out my suddenly flooded emotions.

I returned to the kitchen without paying attention, the corridors already second nature to me, and looked about for something to do. That was the best way to get myself reined in—to keep busy. I'd scrubbed the house until it shone, so that was out. With a flash, I realized we would need bread. Yes, that was it; I would bake bread.

The depleted pantry still contained half a sack-full of flour to work with, and I tipped the covered jars with one finger until I found what I was looking for: the bubbling sourdough. Surprised it was still alive in the manor's murderous temperatures, I separated a small piece and smelled it. Rich, like dirt after rain.

My thoughts stilled as I kneaded, my sleeves folded almost to my elbows and my hands covered in flour. As I had not remembered to pin my hair back up, its waves surged in and out—a chocolate tide—with every pound of my fists.

I covered the dough with a towel and began the impossible task of finding a warm spot in which to let it rise. The few places I found that weren't freezing were still not nearly close to warm enough.

I traveled through the manor, limp dough tucked into a large cloth, and decided, since I'd run out of options, to try outside. Perhaps a puddle of sunshine could be squirmed out of the day.

I stepped out and was almost around the corner before I realized the dark figure kneeling on the trampled snow was Lord Grey. At first, I thought his wrist was bleeding again, but as I looked closer, I recognized the ruby petals. I walked up to him.

"Look."

I flinched. There were weeds everywhere. Their vein-like protrusions tangled up among the rose bushes, suffocating the flowers, oblivious to the threading thorns.

"How did this happen?" I asked.

"I don't know. They were healthy yesterday. This has to be the creature's doing."

Lord Grey's face darkened to match his voice—a lightning storm of hate. He lunged forward and flung his hands into the bush before him, bringing out a deep root. He tore it to pieces, clawing at it until it was green confetti on the snow. He reached for another one, completely ignoring the thorns.

"Sir, stop. Don't you think you've lost enough blood?"

He didn't look at me. I doubt he even heard me.

I tucked the dough against my hip and knelt beside him. "Please, sir." My hand hovered near him, hoping the tug of energies would distract him. It did.

He brought his hands back to his sides. "They were my mother's. She loved them."

"They're not dead, sir. We can still salvage them."

That made him turn to me. "How?"

"We'll cut the weeds. Are there shears anywhere?"

"Yes, I think there are some in the stables."

"Wonderful. Here, sir, hold this." I passed him the soft mound, which he took with all the surprise of a first-time father.

"What—?"

"Just bread, sir, or at least, it will be once I find it a warm spot. For now, our bodies will have to do."

"Wait, it's best if you don't go alone." He rose with a wince and a slight stagger, sending fear through me again, but he merely brushed off his misused trousers.

We walked in silence, Lord Grey still holding the dough, and entered the stable's empty darkness.

Inside, I moved to one side, where there was more light with which to search, while Lord Grey took to the darker edges. I shivered as I remembered how I'd encountered Mr. Keery mumbling in one of those dark stalls. With a jolt, I realized only a few days had passed since that afternoon. It felt like ages ago.

I began moving some items—a bridle, the saddles that looked old and unused—hoping to spy the gleam of shears.

"God Almighty!" Lord Grey exclaimed, making me leap up, my heart already in my throat.

"Sir?"

"The size of some of these rats! For a moment, I thought we'd acquired another horse."

I rolled my eyes, releasing the breath I'd been holding. He seemed to enjoy making me nervous.

I continued with my search, turning up whole masterpieces of cobwebs, but not what we needed. Lord Grey mumbled and cursed as he knocked things about in the gloom, making me grin despite myself. That's precisely why I'd chosen the opposite spot to search.

"Try not to decapitate yourself, sir," I called out after a rather loud thump.

Steps drew near me. "Very amusing, Anne. But look, it appears I am the victorious one."

He held up not one, but two large pruning shears in one of his hands. In the other, of course, he still held the much-jostled dough. He was smiling like a boy who'd just won a race.

"Shall we?"

We spent the rest of the afternoon yanking and slicing the weeds. Lord Grey started a small bonfire, to burn the green menace to ashes, and I placed the dough on a stone next to it, because, well, there was no point in wasting a good flame.

There was a muted quality to the roses while we worked. I had expected the almost physical attack of perfume, yet their scent was as pale as the snow. Many times throughout the strange afternoon, I glanced over at the young man beside me, down in the cold dirt, his clothes a sludgy mess. Despite the blood loss and the morning's trials, his face was lit up with purpose and energy. The thorns that made me jerk back didn't faze him one bit.

Once or twice, when I looked up to feed yet another vine to the fire, I found his eyes on my face, a quizzical look, like a dog hearing a strange noise, quickly disappearing underneath his usual expression. And, as always happened in those tense moments in which my heart took off without my permission, the invisible woman Dora had spoken of hovered before me.

We had almost finished when I began to hear dull clops nearing the house. Lord Grey and I both stood.

"Horses!" I cried.

He wiped his smudged hands over his equally dirty trousers and stepped up to the main path. In a matter of seconds, a small cart appeared, driven by a bloated man with the baldest head I'd ever seen. It was a ruddy chicken's egg.

With a whistle, he brought the horse to a stop.

"My Lord," he said as he huffed and lowered himself to the ground. He didn't appear at all surprised to see the manor's master covered in mud. He was probably used to his strangeness by now.

From where I stood, I could see large sacks resting lopsided against the cart's walls—some brimming over with onions, others with dimpled potatoes. I hoped none of those were for us, since we had enough potatoes to see us through at least a year. Limp chicken bodies tied to one another by their necks peeked out from a crate, along with the hooves of what I thought was a wild pig.

"Hello, John," said Lord Grey.

The man brought down two sacks lumpy with vegetables and another one, which he handed over to me, with a few duck bodies ready to roast.

"I've brought the usual order, my Lord, and also . . ." He rummaged through his pockets until his face cleared. He brought out two crumpled pieces of paper.

"This letter is from Ms. Simple. She asked me to bring it to you, sir." He handed the note over. "And this one is for a Miss Anne Tinning."

With surprise, I took it from him. From the scribble on the envelope, I could see that it was from Elsie. I smiled.

Lord Grey nodded. "Thank you, John. That will be all."

John bowed, making me feel immensely prouder about my own curt-sying, and sighed as he shuffled back up onto his cart. I wondered how such a flimsy looking structure could sustain the girth it transported.

Lord Grey's eyes followed the cart until it disappeared. Then he gave me a sharp look and broke the letter's seal. He began to read it out in a clear voice:

My Lord,

>*I regret to inform you that Peter Keery succumbed to his injuries on the 6th of December. He never regained consciousness, and the doctor had very little hope for his recovery. He will be buried on the 9th. I know you cannot leave the manor, sir, but I thought you should know. Dora and I will remain in Thistle House until we can find another position. I am very sorry, but we cannot return to Rosewood Manor after what has occurred. If you'd be so kind as to mail our references to Thistle House, we would be grateful.*

>*I am sorry to desert my post, one I've had for many years, without proper leave-taking, but I will not of my own free will step foot inside the manor again. I hope his Lordship understands and will forgive a weak woman's fears.*

>*Your most humble servant,*
>*Laura Simple*

My hands had clasped together, crushing Elsie's letter, as the first few words struck me. Mr. Keery was dead. That was two people the creature had erased from this earth; two men who hadn't deserved such a cruel fate.

A laugh slithered out from the flames, low and harsh, making the day many degrees colder. Lord Grey was shaking in anger as the creature laughed.

"That's the last person you've harmed," he whispered to the flames.

"I hardly think so, August. Your pretty little companion is getting to be quite a nuisance."

I felt unseen eyes turn to me from deep in the fire.

"Anne, dear, have you figured out that pesky name yet?" It cackled. "Would you like a hint? I'll tell you what: I promise I'll point you in the right direction when you are minutes from death."

I gathered whatever courage had not been torn apart by the last few days and spoke:

"We'll see about that, wraith."

There was a moment of silence; even the fire appeared to stop crackling. I kept my eyes steady on its orange waves.

"Very good, Anne. August, she's a feisty one. I can see why you fancy her. Nevertheless, she'll be one more limp body when I'm through."

There was a shriek, like ice cracking, and the fire blew out, leaving behind a black plume of smoke twisting in the breeze.

TWENTY-TWO

I DECIDED TO WAIT TO OPEN ELSIE'S LETTER. I didn't want her words marred by Ms. Simple's news. After I calmed down a bit from the shock, I'd be able to give them the attention they deserved.

But even while I prepared our supper, I couldn't shake the feelings that smothered me. Not only was there the weight of grief, but also dread over the wraith's threat. I had no doubt anymore that it would at least attempt to incapacitate me, if not kill me outright.

My hands moved with mindless jerks, taking complete control of the vegetables I was roasting and the rabbits I was slicing to accompany them.

Lord Grey had remained in the kitchen with me while I cooked, ignoring my assurances that I would be fine. As it was, I was more comfortable in the wraith's presence than in the man's. I hated the strange, internal bustling that began whenever I entered his vicinity; it was annoying and disconcerting to my already confused head. Lord Grey, however, seemed to be unaware of my discomfort as he sat at the scarred table, legs drawn up, knees cradling a book. I could barely see his eyes as he dipped in and out of the printed words.

He looked so young and untroubled, oblivious to everything but the story he held in his hands.

"Sir?"

He blinked. "Hmm?"

"I'm going to set the dining table while this finishes roasting."

"No, no. Set the table here. We don't need such a large space, do we?" He didn't raise his eyes off the book.

"All right, sir."

He did look up then. "What? No argument? No discussion about the proper management of the household? I think you're losing your nerve, Anne."

I could only stare.

"I'm teasing, Anne. Do you know what that is?"

"Yes, sir. But I've never been teased by a Lord."

"Ah, well. I suppose I'm not any Lord." His eyes glittered.

I gave him a tight smile. "No, sir. You are not."

He held my gaze for a few seconds, then cleared his throat and returned to his book.

Opening a drawer, I brought out a blue tablecloth, white blooms woven into the fabric like cotton stars. I flung it onto the table with a soft thud and edged around to smooth it out, trying to disturb Lord Grey as little as possible.

Then I brought out silver cutlery for him and pewter for me.

As I was about to place the silver knife on the table, it slipped from my fingers with a light crash. Lord Grey and I both followed our instincts and bent to retrieve it from the floor, each unaware of the other's movements. We thudded heads like two horned animals.

"Damn!" he said, while I just gasped. Apart from the normal pain that followed a bump, we each got a jolt of energy flying through our veins.

I was the first one to start laughing—large gasps that shook my body until I had to kneel on the floor.

Lord Grey stared at me like I'd lost my mind, which, of course, just made me laugh harder. I collapsed against the stones, allowing myself the full release of tension, the full unwinding of tight muscles as bubbling laughter filled me. I shut my eyes and just laughed.

Soon, a crystalline voice added itself to mine and when I peeked, I saw Lord Grey laughing along with me, the knife still clutched in his hands.

Our meal was a merrier affair than the previous night's. We seemed to have stepped through whatever boundary separated us and found ourselves on more comfortable ground.

Lord Grey helped me clear the table, which, really, with only two places settings, was not necessary. As I washed, he seemed reluctant to leave the kitchen, moving chairs around until I had to grit my teeth at the sound.

"I'm concerned about tonight," he said.

"Well, sir, I can't say I'm not."

He kept pacing around the room as I dried my hands.

"What's on your mind, sir?"

"Perhaps it is improper to a ghastly degree, but I think you should spend the night in my chambers."

My eyes widened and I felt all the blood drain from my face. A smile curled his lips.

"Not in that fashion, Anne, for goodness' sake! I mean, you'd be safer, we'd be safer, if we stayed in the same place."

"That would be quite improper, sir."

"I think, in this case, if we follow propriety, one of us will end up dead."

I considered a moment, then shrugged. Little point in holding my honor, whatever that meant, above my life.

"Fair enough."

"You take the bed, Anne, of course, and I'll sleep in the antechamber. I'm sure you're better acquainted than I as to where you might find clean sheets. I'll leave that to you."

"Sir, I couldn't possibly. You're injured and—"

He lifted his arm. "What, this thing? Nonsense. Besides, what kind of brute do you take me for, allowing a woman to sleep in an armchair while I cozy up in my bed? I promise, if I feel myself perishing from lack of comfort, I'll wake you."

The sarcasm was ripe around me. I bit my bottom lip and remained quiet.

With a click, Lord Grey opened the door that led to his actual bedchamber, a room I was curious to see.

It was surprisingly bare, considering how packed with books and objects the antechamber was. His bed was a large, thick creature, solid trunks of wood sustaining a full mattress under a heavy-looking, gold bedcover.

The bed was made, which astounded me. It looked as crisp and tight as if my own experienced hands had tucked it. Lord Grey smiled.

"Yes, the spoiled child knows how to arrange his bedclothes."

I ignored him and continued my conspicuous inspection of the room. A bookcase that brushed the ceiling rested against the back wall, while a matching dresser stood nearby. A desk the color of honey was poised under the only window. There were no paintings or mirrors hanging from the walls, nothing that gave the least bit of personality to the room.

"It's peaceful, sir," I said.

"Yes, I think so. I can't sleep in a cluttered space, I feel like I'm suffocating."

I rounded on his words. "And yet, you're insisting on sleeping in that bedlam out there." I pointed to the antechamber door.

"I really must learn to keep my mouth shut. I'll be fine. I'm tired enough to sleep anywhere."

He opened the dresser's doors like a pair of wings, and brought out a cream film of cloth, plain, and yet, as beautiful a gown as I'd ever seen.

"It would be better if you didn't return to your room tonight. No point in coaxing the creature out. You can use this gown. No one's ever worn it. I bought it as a gift for a . . . an acquaintance, but I never had a chance to give it to her."

My heart froze. Of course, it had to have been meant for Miss Bellingham.

He held the fabric as if he feared it would disintegrate. He placed it on the bed and smoothed out the sleeves.

"You'd be doing me a favor. I feel as if the gown reproaches my neglect. Such beauty should not languish inside a dresser."

Lord Grey raised his eyes to me, deep pools of dark water, regret looking out from the very bottom.

"It's beautiful, sir," I said, my voice catching in my throat.

"It is, isn't it? Well," he said, turning to the door, "if you need anything . . ."

"I know, sir."

He nodded. "I changed my mind about you bolting the doors. I realized last night how foolish that idea was. I give you my word I will not disturb you, and, although I may not be the most trustworthy person, I mean to keep it."

"I trust you, sir."

He lifted one eyebrow at me and shook his head. "Poor Anne, so naive."

I smiled at him despite the sudden darkness that had invaded my mind, and he turned, closing the door behind him without a sound.

I undid the laces on my dress and shoes, feeling my body sigh in relief. I folded my clothes, placing them on the chair by the desk, and turned to the gown on the bed.

It was exquisite. No ruffles weighed it down, no intricate lace strained the eyes, simply a cascade of wheat-colored fabric. I didn't want to put it on, despite its beauty. Not with the knowledge that it had been meant for someone else. Someone loved.

As I picked it up, I wondered what kind of woman it had been meant for. Who could have deserved such delicate beauty? She must have been someone unusual. Most of the fashionable ladies would have considered the gown's simplicity far below their standard. A twinge of that particular darkness twisted in my stomach. It had been meant for a woman special enough to capture Lord Grey's affections.

I frowned at my thoughts. I had no choice in the matter; I'd already agreed. Undoing the line of pearl buttons that reached halfway down the bodice, I lifted it over my head. The fabric seemed to drip down my skin, a touch so light, it felt weightless. With a swoosh of air, it brushed the floor.

There was no mirror in the room, so I moved to the window and pulled back the curtain. Against the black night, I saw my transparent reflection.

My dark hair was stark against the gown, my eyes large. The light gold suited me much more than my old, white dress, which made me look more like a famine victim than a young woman. I attempted to smile at myself without too much success and turned back to the bed, that frightening creature that took up most of the room's space. I brushed the soft bedcover and pulled it back to reveal the crisp sheets underneath.

I pulled the cover from the bed, and removed the used sheets with care. They didn't look like they'd been slept in, which made me wonder how much Lord Grey actually used them, but since I'd already begun, I could change them and be done with it. In the armoire, under a pile of blankets, lay a fresh set that appeared not to have been used in a while. There was a faded lavender satchel tucked into the folds, scenting the linen. Had Lord Grey even known they were in here?

As I brought the sheets out, I felt a square of something solid inside their folds. My hand reached in and pulled the object out. It was a painting, the small image of a woman. Even in the uneven stroke of the artist's brush, I could see the beauty reflecting off her face, a clarity to her dark eyes that drew me in. Her head was cocked slightly to the right, a cascade of auburn hair falling over one shoulder and down the sleeve of her dark wine gown.

"She's lovely, isn't she?"

I gasped as a draft of freezing breath stroked my ear.

"I bet she was even lovelier in person. I never had the chance to see her, unfortunately, but dear August must have gotten quite close to her, don't you think? Enough to keep her portrait in such a private place."

I flinched and backed away from the armoire, away from the voice, even though I knew it could follow me anywhere. Was it the wraith who'd spoken, or my own heart?

"Leave me alone," I murmured.

There was a chuckle. "As you wish, for now. Sweet dreams, little girl." The cold dissipated, until the room was as it had been moments before. Unclenching my fingers from around the picture frame, I placed it back in the armoire, under a heavy blanket, hoping to lock my own thoughts in with it.

I moved to the chair where my everyday gown lay, took the envelope from one of its pockets, and opened it.

The letter was brief—Elsie had never been one for writing—but the paper's scent alone brought me comfort. It smelled like herbs and the soap Elsie preferred.

With a small smile, I started to read:

Dearest Anne,

> *It's been horrid here without you. I miss you something awful, and Mary does too. She pretends otherwise, but I can see her sniffling when she thinks I'm not looking. I've been busy plotting how to get Lady Caldwell to send me over there too. Does your employer need another maid?*

> *It's the strangest thing, sleeping in our room alone. I'm sure you're better off, since my snores are not waking you up at all hours now, but I'm beginning to see that I'm a bit of a coward. Any little noise at night and I hide under the sheets. I never felt like that when you were here. I was always safe with you.*

> *I'm sure you've already made friends with the entire household, but please, if you get a chance, write and tell me how everything is with you. Things must be so much calmer in the countryside.*

> *I'm going to stop now, because the letter is already soggy, but I hope you are well and that they are treating you kindly.*

> *Oh, by the way, have you found that handsome stranger you were looking for? And if so, pray tell me his name.*

> *All my love,*
> *Elsie*

Her words made me smile for an instant, but then my own thoughts twisted that smile into a muffled sob. The ache of missing her mingled with the confusion I felt about everything around me. The manor, the darkness inside it, Lord Grey, the image locked in the armoire . . . nothing was clear or safe. I was lost. Even in my own head. Like my mother, I was paralyzed with fear.

At that moment, what I desired more than anything was to have Elsie next to me, telling me one of her awful jokes.

I folded the letter back up, my hands shaking with silent sobs.

The reality of my situation was a burning pang in my chest.

TWENTY-THREE

I WAS KICKING SOMETHING THAT SLID AROUND me, attempting to brace myself, but finding no foothold. Hands were wrapped tight around my neck; so many hands, pushing their fingers in, digging with their nails. I tried to raise my own to pry them loose, but they wouldn't respond. They were so heavy. I was so heavy, so tired. Water burned my eyes, and I could see my hair waving around me, oblivious to the danger, enjoying the water's caress. I opened my eyes as the hands, the claws, tore at my throat. In front of me, smiling underwater, was a woman, her shining auburn hair encircling me.

With a yelp, I woke. I sat up, my forehead dripping with sweat, and heard that familiar low, crackling laugh.

A second later, Lord Grey was careening through the doorway, his hair a lovely mess. He glanced around the room and then released the tight coil of tension he'd been holding.

"Are you all right?" he asked.

"Yes, sir, just a nightmare."

"Bloody hell, Anne. Do you think you can manage to dream without giving me an apoplexy?"

He shuffled into the room, while I tried to shake the nightmare from my head.

"I'm sorry, sir."

"Sure you are." He moved across the room to the only chair, picking up the clothes I'd left there. I almost didn't catch the care he took in placing them on the desk. As my eyes followed his movements, I saw his hands rest for a second on my gown, one finger tracing the line of black buttons. I frowned.

He pulled the chair forward and sat down, placing his head in his thin hands. I took a moment to check his injury. It looked clean and dry.

"Sir, does it still hurt? Your wrist?"

He looked up. "It's fine. It has stopped . . ." His eyes trailed over me, taking in the gown I was wearing. I began to feel too warm.

"Sir?"

He met my eyes, his face remaining calm and severe. "The gown suits you, Anne."

"Thank you, sir. It is a lovely one."

"I thought so, when I bought it." A red contraction of pain raced through his features and he looked down to the floor. He was quiet for so long, I thought he would not say another word.

My mouth itched to speak the question, to ask about the woman who had followed me into my dreams, but I didn't dare.

Lord Grey cleared his throat and looked back up at me. "It's perfect for you, Anne. Keep it."

"Sir, I couldn't."

"It deserves to be worn, not to hang in a man's closet picking up lint."

I felt myself blushing and I dipped my head, allowing my heavy curls to tumble around me. My heart was beating with painful enthusiasm, sending pulsing thuds up to my throat.

A soft brush of warm air touched a lock of my hair, a caress that sent my hands tingling. I moved and the touch disappeared. Raising my head, I saw Lord Grey was still seated on the chair, his eyes dark and focused on me. Immediately, he lowered them and stood.

"Well, I'll leave you and see if we can both get some more sleep."

"Yes, sir."

He paused, his hand on the doorknob. "It's August, Anne."

He closed the door behind him.

I got no more sleep that night.

"Again, Anne."

He sent a jolt of searing power toward me with a flick of a long finger.

I was standing before him, already bruised and cut, and it wasn't yet mid-morning. Raising my hands, I willed them to become shields, if not weapons, and for a few seconds, I felt Lord Grey's energy pause, held back. I concentrated, but my mind faltered and the anxious wave of power slammed into me, knocking me down.

"Damn it!" I screamed. Rubbing my scraped elbow, I stood.

"That was better, though. It held up a bit longer. I don't think, however, the creature would give you time to gather yourself off the floor."

"Maybe not, but if we keep doing this, I might not make it alive to next week."

Lord Grey's lips twitched. "You have a knack for exaggeration, Anne. But if you're tired, we can try something different."

He walked closer to me and held up his hands. "I will not attack you now. It's your turn. You will attack, and I'll attempt to defend myself." He raised his eyebrows in amusement. "I'm sure this will ease some of your frustration."

He turned around and began walking back across the room. I smiled at the opportunity.

I began to feel that odd sensation of lightness, as if my body were made out of sea-foam and salt, everything around me taking on a sharper feel. The stones felt colder, more grooved; Lord Grey's footsteps were more hollow.

With a deep breath, my blood seemed to warm, bubbling as it thumped down my veins in a thick current. When it became too painful to sustain, I released the power with a sigh.

Lord Grey felt the change in the air and snapped around, his mind raising up a defense that I couldn't see. I felt it deep in my entrails when the energies met, smashing together.

Lord Grey fixed his eyes on mine, and I held the gaze, unblinking, as his reflection wavered like a fish. A flash of pain brushed through his face, and I felt his defenses splinter, then crack. He was thrown backward against the floor, his bones landing with a creaking twist.

The feeling passed in an instant, and I was back in the reality of the main hall, watching as the manor's master bent his torso to sit up.

"That was certainly better," he said.

I attempted to help him, but he waved me off with a trembling hand. "You seem to find it easier to strike first, vicious creature that you are. We need to remember that." He coughed softly and stretched his arm to pick something up off the floor next to him.

"Where did this come from?" He held the object up for me to see.

"Oh, my cross, it must have fallen out of my pocket. Ms. Simple gave it to me."

He turned it over in his hands, the sunlight shining on it. "It can't really protect you, Anne. It has no magic."

I gazed at the small object, then brought my eyes back to him. "Shouldn't something given in affection carry its own brand of magic?"

He stood, walked over to me and handed me the cross. "I don't know. Perhaps."

He didn't back away, but remained close enough for me to feel his warmth playing over my gown. It became harder to breathe.

His cough broke the moment in two.

"I still don't know what to do if the wraith attacks, sir," I said, backing away.

His face darkened as if he'd been pulled back into the shadows.

"August," he murmured.

"Sir, it's not right. I would feel out of place."

"You know, Anne, no one's called me by my given name since my father died. Except for the wraith. I've begun to hate the sound of it. It's one more name I'm trying to recover from the creature's jaws."

When he raised his eyes to me, they were a deep blue, the swirling and shifting colors having subsided.

I couldn't stand that gaze, and I lowered my head. From my throat's recesses, I pulled out the word he wanted to hear, tugging it up by its silver thread all the way to my lips.

"August."

I didn't see his reaction, if there was one. I just kept my eyes on the indifferent stone floors.

"Thank you."

I could only nod.

TWENTY-FOUR

IN THE AFTERNOON, AFTER I'D MANAGED TO
sneak a few cleaning hours to myself, Lord Grey (or August, as I needed
to accustom myself to saying) invited me to a walk around the grounds.

"Well, at least as far as we can make it without puncturing every
artery on rogue branches, or finding ourselves in an uncomfortable
drowning scenario," he said.

I bundled up, rushing into my now glowering old room, my
Bible's residue still floating in the air, and snatched my cloak along
with any other items I might need. I was trying to avoid further trips
to that particular section of the house. It now seemed as much as part
of the wraith's domain as the fountain did.

As if to prove my point, all the doors in the servant's quarter
slammed open at the same time. I gave them a quick look with eyes too
tired to be quaking in fear, and walked back to the front door.

"What was that noise?" August asked.

"The wraith. Obviously, the rooms needed airing."

He looked at me. "You're not afraid, then?"

"I was," I shrugged. "I'm sure I will be again, but for now, I'm willing
to enjoy the day."

He nodded and held the door open as I stepped out of our frozen cocoon and into a cloudy but warming afternoon.

The roses had returned to their naked splendor, and as we passed by them, I caught a smile on August's face.

"Will I ever be able to do that?" I found myself asking.

"What? The flowers?"

"Yes."

He shook his head. "I don't think so, Anne. Your powers are of a different sort than mine, more controlled even in their, as yet, untamed wildness. Not set so much to burst in exuberance as to quiet, to gather together, to calm."

We continued walking around the corner and down toward the stables.

"Summoning, though, I think I could teach you. It's not incompatible with your skills. After all, to banish something, you would need to first call it up."

"I'm not sure that's something I'm willing to experiment with, August."

His voice was suddenly harsh. "Not when you have my example glowing before you."

I stopped. He walked on a few paces, then also stopped. I saw his back, even through his clothing, swaying with the effort it took to avoid one of his coughing spells.

As I looked after him, memorizing every one of his angles, I felt what by then was a familiar dizziness. A stretching root of my thoughts traveled through the snow, over to the dark figure before me. I felt it encircle him, then brush against his skin like soft fur.

August sighed an instant before a lunge of energy nudged me backward.

He turned around. "You were able to reach me, Anne. Very good. You're learning to control it, even to mold it into gentleness. That's something I've never been able to accomplish. My power is violent, and still unpredictable."

He fiddled with the stained bandage around his wrist, pulling at the ragged corners.

"Let me see."

"It's all right. It doesn't hurt."

"Please, August."

He stepped toward me in silence and brought his wrist up to me, pushing back his sleeve.

"May I undo the bandages?" I asked.

"If you can do it without touching my skin."

My hands trembled as I neared them to the linen. I unknotted the fabric, my head bent over the task. Unrolling it, I released the stained skin. Without touching August, I inspected the wound. Still a bit raw, but seeming to be sewing itself back together.

I was so focused on the pale canvas of his arm that I didn't notice the noise until August called my name.

It was the sound of wind caressing feathers, of small, downy chests filled with winter magic floating through the air.

I looked up into a patch of sky that had filled with birds of every sort. Mirror-blue, blood-colored, pupil-black, all of them circling us without a single cry of anger or fear. A harmonious beating of wings. August could not take his eyes off them.

"Birds never come to Rosewood anymore. They sense the darkness that lives here." He smiled. "You've brought the birds back, Anne."

Happiness rushed through me as I realized I had not forced them down into the hard ground. I hadn't attempted to immobilize them.

As I watched, they began to land on the branches all around us, until scaled claws gripped every one of them. We turned to leave them in peace, but a strangled cry pierced through the air. I turned toward the sound and gasped as a laugh encircled me.

On the white ground lay a blackbird, ripped apart, its blood spreading through the snow like spilled wine.

August buried it. I couldn't stand to leave it uncovered like that, for any animal to pick through. After all, the only reason it was dead was because of me.

I couldn't shake the guilt even as we practiced, my lack of concentration chaffing at August until he threw his arms up in silent frustration and sat down right on the floor. I'd never seen anyone who enjoyed cold stone more than he did.

"Unless you'd like to join that little creature in silent death, I think you'd better pull yourself to attention, Anne."

I followed his example and sat down close to him. Almost instantly, I began to feel the tug of energy, like fingers plucking at strings woven deep in my body.

"I don't know if I can do this," I said.

"Do what?"

"This. Help you end all of this. I'm afraid. What if something were to happen, where would I go for help? Would I even be allowed to leave?"

I could feel him turning to look at me as I spoke.

"The wraith can't prevent a Grounder from leaving. It's tied to me and to the manor, not to you. If something were to happen to me, you must grab the essentials and run off the grounds, as fast as you can. Forget about everything but getting yourself past the roses' boundaries."

"And just leave you to die?"

"Yes. I doubt the creature would kill me. Frighten me, yes, but as I told you, it needs me. You, however, will be in danger if I am incapacitated, so leave me to my fate and get out. Is that clear?" His eyes seemed to drill into me.

"Yes, August."

"Look at me."

I raised my face to his.

"Promise me."

"I promise," I said without a twitch. I'd always been a good liar.

We were both in better spirits after a filling dinner, although August left half his plate untouched. I didn't know how he could maintain himself on the little fuel that ran through his veins.

I shooed him away from the kitchen as I prepared his tea, hoping he'd sit and rest a bit, because, in truth, his health still concerned me.

I had just begun to pour the concoction into a cup, smiling in satisfaction as I realized I'd heard August cough less the previous hours, when I heard a trickle of music sliding into the kitchen like a mist of dark notes. I tried to ignore it; I did have things to do, after all. But the music began to fill the kitchen, reminding me of warmth, of grass, of summers in London. I could feel the loosening of muscles as the cold lost some of its power on me. I was putting everything down to follow the music's trail, when a breath of pure voice surprised me, twined around the piano's lament.

The music grew as I neared the parlor, edging into the doorway and gazing at a sight that made me smile.

August had pulled off the white cloth that had covered the large, black piano, and he was sitting at its bench, almost completely bent over its keys. His voice was not the strongest I'd ever heard—it was tremulous like a flower in a sudden rain shower—but it was clear.

He sang on, in Italian, from what I could tell with my limited ear, never lifting his eyes off the keys before him. I yearned to get close and yet, I hated to break the crystalline moment of peace the room cradled.

His voice lifted in flight, and my feet began to move toward him, as if they had their own thoughts on the matter. I felt an irresistible current passing through me, leading me on to what my future was holding.

August still did not look up as I stood near the crook of the piano, attempting not to mar its fluid surface with my touch. He sang on, his voice wrapping around me, its feathery caress soft, light.

The silence was so vast when he finished, that I dared not utter a single compliment. I stood where I was, tension wrapped tightly around me.

Many moments passed. And then August rose from the bench with such decision, he frightened my heart into a gallop. He came to stand before me, only a sliver of air separating our bodies. I couldn't look up into his face, for fear, for shame, for a hunger that twisted and boiled in my stomach. Our energies brushed against each other in a painful tangle.

I saw August's hand lift from his side and come close to my face. His skin never touched mine, never touched my hair, and yet I felt the warm caress nonetheless, like a silken flame that yearned to burn everything near it. I closed my eyes with an intake of breath, feeling his other hand close to my right arm, my gown's fabric shimmering as his fingers hovered above it, and trailed down to my hand.

I opened my fingers with unconscious yearning. I could almost feel his thin ones wrapping around mine, clutching at them in aching panic.

When I thought I couldn't stand the tension anymore, it stopped. As my heart slowed down and my blood cooled like tea, I opened my eyes.

August had disappeared.

He paced through most of the night. I could hear him like a distant drum as I came in and out of a crackling layer of sleep.

An itching worry slept next to me. We were still missing the crucial piece, and I had a feeling things were about to escalate.

A most accurate premonition.

TWENTY-FIVE

AUGUST'S VOICE WAS AS COLD AS THE STONES around us as he passed me a sheet of paper etched with strange words. I took it with trembling hands, eyes fixed on anything that wasn't the man in front of me.

"You need to learn this. You are ready, so we will attempt what we've discussed tomorrow. We need to be prepared for the second we know the master's name. The wraith will give you no time when that moment comes. It will destroy you to save itself." He pointed at the black words. "This is a banishing chant, one I've come across in my studies, and the one that is the strongest for destroying this particular creature. I have divided the chant, since it's usually performed by only one person. You will say these words here, and I will say the ones at the bottom. This blank space here, in my part, is where the blasted name goes."

I flinched at his tone. "I thought magic was written in those strange symbols." I indicated the tiles beneath us.

"These words are the symbols written phonetically. I could hardly expect you to learn a new language in a day. We'll read them through together a few times, mainly to show you were the accents go, and then you must learn them. Memorize them."

We stood there, as awkward as was humanly possible, and read through the knotted words. He corrected my clumsy attempts, picking apart the tangled consonants until the vowels shone through with resonant clarity.

When I was able to run through my whole part without faults, August sighed.

"Good. Now, I want you to forget everything else today. I don't want to see a single dust rag in your hands, just this piece of paper. You need to know this well enough to chant it when faced with any atrocity the wraith will create for us. These words need to roll off your tongue, full of power and without a single stammer, or we're both lost. Do you understand?"

He looked up at me fully for the first time that morning. His eyes were dark, an almost velvet brown. I couldn't hold his gaze.

"I understand."

"All right." He turned around and headed back up the stairs in silence.

I found I was swimming in a deep pit of disappointment, which made me realize I had actually been expecting something to change between us. I hated feeling the twist of nerves in my stomach, a warm acid that swelled whenever August approached. It had come into existence with such subtlety, such quiet steps, I hadn't noticed how strong its grip on me was until this very moment.

August's words, so cold and indifferent, had left me emptied out, as if someone had carved me like a pumpkin. Had I imagined the tense moment the night before? Had I mistaken friendliness for an affection even I didn't understand? Maybe Miss Bellingham, whoever and wherever she was, truly did still have a hold of his heart. Maybe he was waiting to be rid of this wraith to return to her, and I was just the one who'd help set him free.

I'd never been in love, had never come anywhere near it, so I couldn't tell which part of me was bleeding, my pride or my heart. Was this how Dora had felt all that time, as if she'd swallowed fire?

It all needed to end. We (a confusing word) needed to destroy the creature and get on with our lives, whatever that meant for him. For me, it would mean picking up dirt on a daily basis. Back to what I was used to.

Why, then, did the thought leave me breathless?

I sat at the dining table and focused on the words.

With "Alchroth," the first word in the chant, I had to make sure the "ch" was pronounced as "k," and that the vowels were pure. Having no idea what the words could mean, I memorized them by rote, learning the first two words, then adding a third, then going back to the beginning and trying again. I wrote them down as I spoke them.

The creature was near. I could feel it, ducking behind me, breathing against my back, doing everything it could to crack my delicate concentration.

Finding myself under the protective mirror's gaze, its hum a blanket of sound around me, I felt little fear, only the cold becoming a serious nuisance as the minutes wore on. Finally, it spoke.

"Anne, why are you going to all this trouble?"

I ignored its words and kept reading.

"You know he's just using you to get what he wants. You must realize I can't allow that to happen. He's risking your life, and he doesn't even care for you. You could never fill his heart, you silly girl."

I held myself still, not allowing my pain to show.

The wraith cackled, making me shiver.

"Do you really believe you can defeat me? I can smell your fear. Maybe August was right, and you are nothing more than a maid."

I flinched as I remembered the moment the wraith spoke of.

"This is the last warning I will give you, Anne. The next time we meet, you'll be seconds from death. Think about that, sweet girl, while you stamp those words into your mind. They will be useless to you when your blood soaks the floor. We are done playing, Anne."

The current gave my shoulder a push and then left.

"We never were," I said to the empty room.

August didn't come back down until dinner time, and by then, I was so lost in the strange words that I barely registered his presence. He nursed a cup of tea between his hands as he sat down in front of me.

I kept my eyes on the paper that was wrinkled and stained, although the concentration had left me as soon as his soft scent brushed up to my nose. Maybe if I kept my gaze lowered, he would leave me be.

Of course, no such thing happened.

"Have you memorized the words?"

"I think so."

"You better be surer than that if you attempt to help me."

I don't know why the asperity in his voice irked me as much as it did. He'd spoken to me in that fashion before, and I had no reason to believe he wouldn't continue to do so in the future.

"Perhaps I shouldn't, then," I said.

His laughter was a vicious thing, full of teeth and claws.

"Then what, may I ask, are you still doing here?"

"I don't know."

"Perhaps you should leave, then."

My head spun as I rose from my seat with a gust of cloth. "Perhaps I should, *sir.*"

I spat the last word at him and left the room.

I slammed into my old room, ignoring the cold and the decisively unforgiving atmosphere. I would be damned if I retreated to the master's rooms again.

In those first few moments, I was prepared to leave by foot to another manor, to anywhere that didn't smell like roses or carry cold like a shawl on its shoulders. Anywhere away from him.

But reason took over as my tired mind stopped banging about my head. I could do no such thing, of course. For one, I had very little money, no references, and, in all honesty, I didn't fancy traveling through the forest on foot just as the sun was setting. No, I had to remain and face whatever was coming.

Sighing, I went back to the kitchen to put together a dinner I was sure neither of us would eat.

I carried the covered dishes to the dining room, afraid of finding August still sitting there, but not quite relieved when I didn't. I sat at the table and took up the words again, finding a vague comfort in their sounds.

An hour later (an hour of waiting that dug itself deep as a splinter into my chest), he still hadn't come to eat. The room was dark, almost in complete darkness, and I had been unable to read the lines before me for long minutes.

I shrugged and returned to the servant's quarters.

The last thing on my mind was sleep, even after all the disrupted nights. I shuddered at the idea of lying still. I wondered if this was how August felt every day, that unquenchable shifting of energy that made him who he was.

I lit the lamp on my night table and leant my silver cross against it. Kicking my shoes off, I sat down on the bed.

A name. It all came down to a name. Tomorrow, I would face that creature to wrestle it from its jaws. I wondered if I'd be able to before it killed me.

Shaking my head in an attempt to also shake my fears away, I began to chant to myself, growing calmer as the words came to my lips with ease, frowning when one would stick to my tongue, sending me fumbling. I kept thoughts away by humming, filling my head with noisy minutia until not a single, fat thought could squeeze in.

I spent two hours in an almost trance-like state as I hummed or whispered to myself.

My body finally began to sway with sleep.

I had just placed the crumpled paper in my pocket for safekeeping and was pulling back my bed's covers when the knock sounded against my door. A whisper of knuckles that made me shiver.

I don't remember walking to the door, but I must have because I suddenly found the doorknob in my hand, turning in my shaking palm.

He was barely visible in the gloom. His face was veiled in shadows, yet I felt the familiar tug of his eyes on mine.

"I'm sorry, Anne. I thought it was the right thing, pushing you away. Forgive me, it's not."

He reached out, past my face, and I felt the weight of my freed hair as it tumbled down.

His hands lay with a hesitant flutter on its waves. And then his fingers plunged in, cupping the base of my head. I gasped at his touch. He kissed me, swallowing the pain and matching it with his own as our lips became torches, fighting against each other.

August's arms clasped around me, dragging out a low moan from his throat. I felt like I couldn't catch my breath, everything in me ached and vibrated, the buzzing of blood filling my ears as my heart crashed against my ribs in a panic I didn't understand.

We were pressed so close, burning so tightly, that there was not a single edge of my skin that was not as alive as it had ever been. His thin arms pressed against my body with such urgency. His rose scent was as overwhelming as when I'd first stepped into the manor's grounds.

I didn't want to release him.

From somewhere behind me, a noise began, a growl that seemed to seep into my very skin, digging down into my bones until every part of me echoed with the sound.

I didn't have time to do anything but gasp as a frozen claw wrenched me backward. There was nothing, then.

Nothing but darkness.

TWENTY-SIX

THE POUNDING IN MY HEAD BROUGHT ME BACK up to consciousness. I opened my eyes to a tight darkness that pressed against me. My body was stiff and frozen, but my head was screaming in pain.

I attempted to sit up, only to roil in dizziness. I stopped and moved again, a bit slower, inching my body up layer by layer until I was upright. My hand went up to my head, and I winced at the stinging my fingers produced. They came away wet with a slick blackness that could only be blood.

What had happened? I couldn't recall anything past . . .

My skin warmed at the memory of burning arms, of a wave of dark hair against my brow. My skin felt raw where it had touched August's, but I smiled in the dark at the sweet discomfort. Taking a look around, I realized I was sitting on the floor, that I'd most likely been lying there for a while if my stiffness could be trusted.

I stood, allowing my eyes to adjust to the darkness, and I saw I was still in my room. A glitter on the floor told me the whereabouts of my lamp, now many sharp pieces scattered on the wooden boards.

Beside them, there was a twisted lump of metal.

Oh, no.

I bent down and picked up what had been my cross, now, nothing more than a shapeless, sad thing. Cursing under my breath, I moved to the door, which was wide open. I leant against it so my unsteady legs could relearn to sustain me, and felt something wet under my bare feet.

A jolt rose up my legs to my chest, and my breath was swallowed up by a gasp.

August.

The last few seconds before I'd been knocked unconscious flashed through my head. A scream of fury, a growl twisted by hate, a wall of frozen air flinging me backward, away from August's arms. My hand brushed the door and felt another slick streak of dark liquid.

The pain forgotten, I broke into a run through the hallways I knew so well, my feet thumping to my heart's rhythm.

"August!" My voice echoed against the walls, his name thrown back at me in cold mockery. I ran through the empty hallway, a shriek flying past me, lighting all the lamps that hung like insects from the wall. I gasped at the sudden brightness.

"Anne." A shadow edged into my view—a tall, thin figure that moved without sound.

"August?" I whispered.

He stepped into the light and gave me a smile. "Why are you running?"

"I found blood in my room. You weren't there, and I—"

He shrugged, his eyes never swerving from mine. "You thought you had to come to my rescue." His smile widened. "How sweet."

He stepped closer, his smile still glinting in the lights.

"I didn't know—"

"Of course you didn't. How could you? But see, there's no need to worry. I'm just fine."

He did seem fine, but I still felt on edge, my nerves stretching thin. "I'm glad you're all right, but what happened?"

He shrugged again. "You know, I have no idea. I woke up in the main hall, sprawled on the floor, freezing and very stiff."

"So did I, except in my bedchamber."

His eyes were frozen on mine, his smile widening into an uncomfortable size. "Well, there's little point in worrying over that now—I know the name. The wraith let it slip."

I clutched my hands together. "That's wonderful!"

"Yes, it is. I think we should get started on what we were planning, don't you agree, Anne? We don't have much time."

Cocking my head, I shifted on my feet, willing the squirming in my stomach to subside. "Yes, of course, August. I'm ready."

Would he say anything about what happened in my room, or would he ignore it? I supposed we had more important things to worry about, but it was still peculiar he hadn't at least been sarcastic about it.

"Good," he said. "Come on, then. I have to pick up a few supplies from my room. You can help me bring them down to the dining room."

August turned around and moved down the corridor as I smiled and followed him. That man was so strange.

Half-way down the etched hall tiles, he paused, a shiver rippling through his body.

"August?" I stepped closer. I was about to lay a hand on his shoulder when I felt something that stilled my movement. The energy pulsing beneath my palm was not the usual flaming push, but one that needled my skin with ice. Under our feet, the symbols carved into the stones began to glow.

I shut me eyes and took in a breath.

"You're not August." My voice was calm, my thoughts gathering, pulling back toward my center like the receding tide. I opened my eyes to a profile that was morphing into a mask of hate.

"What gave it away?" the wraith asked.

"You can change your features, but not your energy."

The now unrecognizable face smiled. "Clever girl."

The wraith lunged at me, losing shape, becoming mist. It was made of slivers of glass, and I screamed as it swallowed me, blood blooming throughout my body.

My hand warmed in anger and I struck out with a strangled shriek. The creature retreated for a second, which was all I needed. I burst into a run, down the hall.

"August!" I screamed as I took the stairs two at a time, my bare feet sure on the steps. "August!" I threw open his door, taking in the scattered objects, the ripped books, the unhinged bedroom door. The bitter smell of smoke wafted through the air, obliterating any scent of the herbs that lay scattered on the floor. I didn't see fire or its remnants anywhere, but its presence was unmistakable.

"That is a familiar smell, isn't it, Anne?" A low voice, one I didn't recognize, said from behind me. "I've been waiting for you to wake. We have a few things to discuss, the two of us."

I turned and felt my stomach drop. It couldn't be.

Lily Bellingham stood before me, a curling smile on her perfect, porcelain face. She looked just like she had in August's memory, her beauty as overwhelming as the roses' scent.

She nodded once. "I trust you know who I am?"

"But . . . you died! You killed yourself!"

"That is a yes, then." She folded her gloved hands in front of her moss green gown. "No, pathetic girl, it is obvious that I did not die. It is not hard to feign one's death at night in the middle of London, especially when there is no one left to identify one's body. Which, thank to August's murder, was exactly the case." She chuckled, a dry, low sound. "Quite easy to accomplish, actually."

I took a step forward, my eyes looking past the doorway through which she'd just appeared. She'd been waiting for me inside his bed-chamber. "Where is he?"

"That is not your concern." She moved a hand in a graceful sweep and the wraith's freezing presence was suddenly in the room with us.

My eyes widened as the truth finally settled in my head. "It was you! You're its master."

"Of course I am, Anne. I'm a little hurt neither of you even considered it, although, perhaps I shouldn't be, not with everything August did to me all those years ago. He obviously thought I was too stupid, too worthless, to be taken seriously."

"What are you talking about? He loved you!"

Her laughter was a dark, harsh sound. "Love, Anne, doesn't exist. That is one thing that August made sure to teach me."

The smell of smoke was getting stronger by the second. I had to find him. "Where is he? Tell me!"

Lily Bellingham snapped her fingers, dragging my attention back to her. "You will listen, Anne, through your own free will, or my substantial one."

Icy fingers pressed against my jaw, keeping my head turned toward her.

She smiled. "Good. Where was I? Oh, right. August never took my powers seriously. I can't say I truly blame him, though, since my own father dismissed them, considering magic far above a woman's reach. Quite a laugh, isn't it, that I outlived him and all his precious Brothers? I'm the only magician left in London, now. And young Lord Grey was such an easy target. While the police scrambled about, trying to find who could have possibly killed all those men at the same time, I set the wraith on him, even ordering it to whisper its own conjuration in his ear so that the poor man would think it was the luck of the draw that brought it into the house."

I blinked, trying to make sense of the violent woman in front of me, one who looked nothing like the kind, bright person in August's memories. "So this is all revenge, then?"

"Of course."

"But it was an accident! Your father tried to kill August!" I tried to shake myself loose from the freezing magical fingers, but they just dug into my flesh, keeping my head where it was. If I could only concentrate, I'd be able summon my own energy to battle hers, but I couldn't get my mind to remain still enough.

Lily's crystalline eyes seemed to glow as she watched me. "I would like to show you something, Anne. The truth August has so carefully tucked away from you. Since you won't outlive this night, probably not even this hour, this will be the only chance I have to show you what kind of man he really is."

She lifted her arms, her gown's fabric shining in the candlelight, and clapped her hands together. When she separated them, an orb so bright it seemed to burn my eyes hovered above her palms.

"Look," she said.

I tried to look away, anywhere but the orb, but it was impossible. The light called to me, and I obeyed.

Everything around me was disappearing, just as it had when I'd looked into August's mirror.

How long I fell was impossible for me to know, but I finally crashed into the ground, my hands braced to keep my head from hitting the hard floor.

I groaned.

Dark, velvet-thick laughter surrounded me as I tried to stand. I was in Rosewood's sitting room, or at least, I thought I was, because the walls twisted, darkening and brightening, the furniture changing position each time I looked away. Was this what it was like in Lily Bellingham's head?

"August, what is the matter?" Her voice came from somewhere in the room around me, though it kept moving as much as the furniture. I narrowed my eyes against the pulsing darkness and was finally able to make out two figures sitting on a sofa. Even if she hadn't spoken his name, I could have recognized that thin silhouette anywhere.

Using a side table that I hoped wouldn't decide to scurry away, I pulled myself to my feet. My hand brushed something soft and I looked down. It was the sleeping gown, the one August had given me to wear, carefully folded in an opened box that wavered in and out of focus, as if her mind couldn't quite remember what it had looked like.

"August, please," Lily said.

"There's nothing more to say, Lily. I cannot offer you anything, certainly not what you assumed I meant when I asked you to come to Rosewood for the summer. I cannot marry you. I don't even love you."

My eyes widened.

The room's walls turned a dark red, as if they had been painted with blood, and the air became even colder than it had been. A whimper stained the stillness.

This couldn't be normal. Lily's head was wrong, her memories twisted by anger, perhaps even by madness.

"But I thought you did, August. I thought we were meant to be together. All that time we spent speaking of magic, of our futures here in Rosewood."

"I am sorry if I misled you. I enjoyed our conversations, but they did not mean as much to me as you thought they did. We are friends, nothing more."

There was a growl from somewhere nearby.

"You used me," Lily said. Her voice held no expression.

"I did not mean to."

"You befriended me to remain in good standing with my father. To move up the ranks of magicians."

"I admit it may have started that way, but that's no longer the case. I consider you a friend."

"Liar."

August sighed and said again, "I am sorry if I've misled you."

She shook her head, and though I couldn't see her face, I knew, by the room's sudden shaking, that she was laughing.

"Oh, August," she said. "You are not sorry. But you will be. I promise you."

Icy hands gripped my hair and pulled me through the dark room, flinging me back into the present, where Lily waited.

"Do you see now, Anne? Do you comprehend why I had to do what I did? He deserves it." She smiled. "You should be glad. He's used you, as well, keeping you close to him to fight the wraith, but what would happen if, by some miracle, you were successful? Do you think he'd remain by your side when he no longer needed you?"

Her words bit into me. The same doubt I'd felt just this morning rose up in me, a living, squirming thing that I wished I could smother. "It is not the same."

Lily laughed and nodded. "You're right, it is not. It is worse for you, dear, for you are just a servant."

"I know August."

"Do you, now? Why did I have to show you that particular memory, then? You should have known all about it. After all, that little scene was why he felt he had to leave the Brothers. He was too much of a coward to remain in my society after his confession."

It was true. He hadn't told me why he'd decided to leave The Order, what had been the catalyst that had started this whole horror. He should have said something.

"That's right, Anne. He betrayed you as much as he betrayed me."

The wraith, which had remained by her side until then, slithered toward me, its harsh chuckle making me shiver as much as the cold. "Anne, Anne, Anne," it hissed.

I took a step backward. "Stop it."

"Face the truth, dear."

I couldn't have been that blind, that infatuated. He couldn't have tricked me that easily.

August's face flashed through my mind: the smiles he'd given me, rare, but brilliant; his worry at my well-being; the feel of his arms around me; the trust he'd placed in me.

I pushed aside everything Lily had said and rifled through my own memories as I tried to beat back the rising panic. One moment glowed, its unmarred light making it stand out. It was the moment in the kitchen, when we'd hit our heads trying to grasp the fallen knife. The carefree way he'd allowed himself to laugh and the warmth I'd felt while I watched him. Despite everything that had been happening around us, we'd found a spot of peace, a moment of happiness.

Something inside me snapped.

Whatever Lily said, whatever she showed me, it didn't matter, because I loved him. I loved August.

The sudden knowledge spread warmth through my entire body, pushing everything else aside.

I loved him, and I wanted him safe even if it meant I'd been a fool. I was not Lily. I would not hurt him just because I'd been hurt. Love went beyond that, it *had* to, or it wasn't worth a speck of dust.

My eyes met hers. "We *will* end you *and* your wraith."

Her smile vanished at my words. She'd been so sure she had me. "I rather doubt you'll have enough time, my dear."

I realized the burning smell had begun to grow into an almost physical presence while we spoke. A dim glow caught my eyes, coming from the window. I crossed the room and gasped.

A trickle of fire was spreading along the outer walls, following the roses' path as they bordered the manor.

"I had hoped you would change your mind. Despite what you might think, I don't revel in killing innocent people, but I see you've made your choice." She nodded to the swirling mass that was the wraith. "I'll leave you to it, then." She flung the door open and disappeared.

Let her leave. I couldn't worry about her now, not when I had to find August and get us out before the flames made it impossible. The manor was made of stone, but the inside was gilded with wooden panels and furniture that could easily lure the fire, creating a trap for anyone left inside. I ran out of the room and careened down the hallways.

"August! Damn it, August!"

Nothing but the growing hiss of the flames licking the stone walls. Gripping the banister that would soon enough be no more than ashes, I took the stairs in a few leaps and ran to the servant's quarters for my shoes. Not bothering with stockings, I fastened them on and started off toward the main hall again.

"August!"

"He's not in the house, stupid girl," the wraith hissed. Its voice's cadence was so much like Lily's that I had to make sure she wasn't still nearby. How had August not recognized it? "Why would I let him burn when he is the one who provides me with the energy I need? I thought you were brighter than that."

I stood my ground, refusing to be cowed. "Then why did you attempt to kill him days ago, huh? Or did you forget that little incident?" My words were much steadier than I had expected.

"If I had wanted to kill him, I would have. Another thread of sliced skin and his life would have ebbed out in a pool of blood. But I would not make it so easy for him. No. My master wants him weak and alone."

Enough pleasantries. The smoke was beginning to crawl down my throat, tickling a passage that threatened to clamp down in a cough.

I reached for the doorknob. I hadn't expected it to be open, so I was not surprised when all my yanking produced was nothing more than vague creaks in the massive wood.

"Bastard," I muttered.

Laughter broke out again, followed by a shriek of agony that multiplied against the walls.

I realized that the screams were coming from the roses. As impossible as it seemed, their voices were raised in fear and pain as their petals sizzled and curled. I held my hands over my ears to block the sound out, but the voices were inside my head. Unstoppable.

I needed to get out. Not bothering to test the kitchen door, since I knew enough of the wraith's and Lily's intelligence, I threw my attention to the large windows. Some of them had stone bars through them, which meant I wouldn't fit, but two of them did not.

The main hall had nothing heavy enough to throw, so I went into the dining room and yanked up one of the chairs, dragging it back with me. It was heavy and massive and would break through the panes without problem.

I raised it up, shouldering its weight and flung it forward with as much force as I could muster.

The blow was deflected, an invisible barrier crashing against the chair, breaking it in a multitude of limp pieces.

"No!"

"I don't know what you take me for, Anne, but I can assure you, I'm not stupid. I wouldn't bother trying the other windows."

I threw myself against the door, pulling at it, rattling its heavy boards. I knew I couldn't break it.

"Damn it."

What could I do? What options were left to me?

The crackling was growing louder, ferocious in its triumph, while the roses grew weaker. I could attempt to stop the fire with my power, but I had no clue if it would work against such an assault. This was not what August had prepared me for.

An idea jolted me out of my racing thoughts.

I felt my blood tremble with excitement. Yes. Yes, it could work.

TWENTY-SEVEN

I RAN BACK TO THE KITCHEN AND GRABBED everything I could find that would work as kindling. There wasn't much more than some old newspapers, but I was sure it would be enough. I added the box of matches to the pile in my arms and a cloth I'd soaked in a bucket of water left over from the washing.

I could feel the creature's eyes on me, trying to weigh my arms down, to stop me in my tracks, but I just smiled and continued on into the main hall and up to the front door. I deposited the crumpled paper on the floor and took a deep breath.

"What are you doing?" The voice was harsher than I'd ever heard it, but there was an edge to it, like a frayed hem, that betrayed a different emotion than anger. Could it have been fear?

I pulled out a match, feeling the wood crisp against my fingers, and struck it hard against the box, igniting it.

"You stupid girl, what are you doing?"

I didn't turn. "You wanted fire? You've got it."

I held the match against the newspapers, allowing the flame to caress them, to grow into them. The glow was reflected on the door's wooden panels.

"I could have arranged a quicker death, if that's what you wanted."

"Oh, you know very well that is not my intention. Or are you stupid enough not to realize the front door is made of wood?"

I raised the soaked cloth up to my face as the smoke increased.

The wraith tried to rush past me in a clumsy attempt to stop the fire, but I rounded on the invisible current.

"What are you planning to do? You can't snuff it out; I created it, and you have no power over it. As far as I know, the only Grounder in the room is me." I struck out with my empty hand, concentrating all the tingling warmth I felt into a tight ball. The creature jerked back with an echoing yell.

If someone had asked me right there how I'd managed to create an energy ball, I would have been as confused as the wraith was, but I didn't question my instincts, on the contrary, I allowed them to take over my shaking body.

The smoke grew and mingled with that coming from outside until I had to blink back burning tears. The door was disappearing under a blanket of flames, but would it be quick enough?

The wraith's screaming was becoming unbearable, a taunting screech that seemed to pummel my ears. I began to whimper with pain, not sure how much longer I could keep myself upright under the assault of sound.

When I heard the telltale crackling, the welcomed noise of wood collapsing, I neared the door. I caught a peek at the snow, stained with the fire's light, and I smiled. Just a little more.

Yanking down another curtain, aware of its thickness and length, I wrapped it in many loops around my body. I stood still, or attempted to, as the wraith slammed its currents against me in a vain attempt at intimidation. I was too scared to be scared.

With a swoon, a large, half-chewed piece of door collapsed, and I saw my opportunity. I wrapped the cloth even tighter around myself and, with a deep breath, ran at the smoldering outline that was the door.

I crashed through it, accompanied by a furious shriek. I landed hard against the ground and immediately sloughed off the curtain that was trailing flames. Pressing some snow on a few ignited locks of my hair, I checked that no other part of me would be eaten by the orange fire.

The outside air was bitter, sour, and smelling of rot. Looking around, I realized there were no roses left, they'd all disappeared under the murdering blanket that covered the houses' facade. I could hear window panes bursting, scattering glass into the manor's frightened floors. There would be very little left come morning, but that was not my concern. No, I had to find August.

I rounded the house and saw the stables also burning, the hay in the stalls making the fire's job that much easier. I only had time to give a silent thanks that there had been no horses in there before what felt like a burning, icy manacle gripped my left wrist and threw me to the ground. My skin was bubbling in pain; the wraith's energy was at least twice August's.

The creature snarled as it yanked me forward, dragging me through the frozen ground while I attempted to gain my footing. I braced myself, pulling my arms back, but to no avail. My strength was nothing against the invisible force.

All I could do was scream and make as much racket as I could so August could hear me. As a twisted root dug into my ribs, I realized where the wraith was taking me and my limbs seemed to turn to powder. Where was August?

The trees' shadows appeared before us, opaque and silent, and inside their shadows lay my nightmare. I could hear the bubbling with its guttural gargle, spitting out black water that was as heavy as stone.

"No," I moaned, kicking my legs, knowing it would do nothing.

There was a barking laugh and a slap of air against my face.

"Since fire didn't work, let's try water," the voice whispered into my ear, then screamed nonsense into the air.

As it dragged me through two of the sentinel trees, I caught a large shadow at the fountain's feet—a dark, long puddle of fabric and . . .

"August!" I yelled.

He lay immobile on the snow.

"Don't worry your little head, he's alive. Don't know if he'll be able to walk again, though."

I looked at August's legs, one of which lay at an awful angle. My eyes dried at the sight of his crumpled body, tossed like a used napkin on the floor.

The pain around my wrist increased, cutting through my skin until the cold seemed to freeze the bone underneath. I had to do something. I had to get loose.

I stopped flailing and screaming, growing as limp as August's body, and took a deep breath. The smell of pine trees mingled with the flow of words in my head, words that, in my panic, I'd forgotten I even knew.

I began a steady chant, concentrating on that glowing orb in my center, creating a golden thread that spun around me and around the creature that held me, slowly tightening around its own grip on me.

I felt the manacle loosen, and I increased my chant's speed, weaving it faster and faster and tighter and tighter until the bond was almost non-existent. That's all I needed. I jerked my hand back, gasping as the cold night air invaded the raw skin, and scrambled to my feet as the wraith snarled and roared.

What now?

I wouldn't have too much time before it came up with another way of destroying me. I ran to August and knelt down.

"August! Wake up! August!"

I shook him, but only managed to release a moan of pain.

"August, it was Lily! She is the wraith's master!"

The swirling air behind me alerted me to the wraith's attack, and I swung an arm toward the current, making it ripple with my power.

As I brought my hand down to my side, I felt a crinkling in my pocket. I'd taken out the cross and substituted it with . . . my breathing grew fainter as I realized what it was. I drew it out with shaking hands and unfolded the wrinkled paper. Yes! Yes! The chant, complete with August's part. I clutched at it and spoke his first word in a thick, fear-choked voice.

"Riethalon!"

The wraith seemed to pause and listen as I repeated the first word. It chuckled.

"Quite pathetic, Anne. You shouldn't tangle with things you know nothing about."

I repeated my chant, which seemed to lend me protection for a short period of time, until I could figure August's part out.

The memory of his voice filled my head as I tried to decipher the words, the rules bouncing and echoing in his cold voice. There were so many I didn't know! And the accents, how would I know where they went?

The wraith laughed and laughed, breaking my grasping concentration.

"Give it up, little girl," its sing-song voice said.

TWENTY-EIGHT

THE CREATURE BEGAN TO CIRCLE ME AS MY protective chant ebbed away, the golden glow shrinking around me while my mind was still on the paper in my hands.

The words were fleeing from me, scattering in all directions. I spoke August's first line, hazarding the wrong accents, hazarding everything. I had no other option. Before I could get to the second line, a stab of pain whipped around my stomach in a tight knot that twisted with every breath.

The wraith laughed and continued its circling. "That's what happens when you meddle with magic. Mispronounced words strike back. Didn't your master teach you that?"

The cramp eased, but I knew I couldn't afford to try the unknown words again. The wraith would take advantage of the spasms and kill me without trouble. Clutching the paper in my hands, I steadied myself. A deep breath to smooth out my nerves, a dip of my head to gather my shredded thoughts. For all I knew, I would die that very night at the foot of a black fountain, next to the man I'd be leaving in a frozen purgatory until his death.

Everything in me sharpened at that thought, at giving my life up with such ease, at giving August's life up when it was not mine to sacrifice.

This was what I had been born for. Not to become my father, content to mindlessly serve, or my mother, to yank at binding chains, but to be this woman. This person willing to fight for what she wanted. My heart, not my supposed destiny, had led me to this instant, to this death-soaked moment, and I would not betray it that easily.

My head filled with the screams of birds, a shrill chorus that returned my chant's words back to me.

I began to speak once again as I edged closer to August's limp body. Repeating the only words I knew, the protective ones that comprised my part of the banishment, I encircled us both with my voice. I would keep going until I couldn't anymore, and then, well, there was nothing more I could do.

The wraith stopped its movement, and settled into banging its energy against the walls of the golden circle, slamming over and over into it, until I could feel the pressure even in my chest. I ignored it and raised my eyes to the sky above me, to the silent, peaceful stars that freckled the night with their light, and just chanted, my gaze fixed on their glow.

I don't know for how long I maintained it. Long enough to grow tired. I could feel it already, a slight trembling in my limbs as the energy required to maintain the circle started draining me. My eyes blurred with exhaustion, but still I chanted, even as pain filled my body.

A sudden sound almost cracked my shell of concentration. A thin, weak voice trickled in, twining around my own.

My eyes widened at the muted but familiar voice, and I glanced down at August, who was struggling to sit up, wincing and shaking with pain. His voice was speaking the words I'd so struggled with.

The wraith growled in hot fury and rammed its energy into my shield, making me stagger backward. I felt a hand brush my skirt, calling my attention with its damp burn. August extended his hand toward my own.

Everything seemed to be slower than it truly was. I could almost see the air particles around me, as crystalline as drops of the coldest water.

I sank with a sigh of fabric to the snow next to August. His eyes locked on mine and he grasped my hands in his. The power coursed through us, through our blood, through our joined skin until I felt we would rise off the ground.

The wraith screamed and crashed against the ever-stronger shield, while August's magic chipped away piece after piece of the creature's malevolent being.

It was all too much. My body swayed with the effort and the pain; my breath came faster, crowded with words, out of my mouth.

August shook my hands and forced my drooping eyes back on him. I answered his unasked question with three words: "Lily! Lily Bellingham!"

His eyes widened, but he didn't hesitate, trusting me completely as he lifted his voice into a shout. I joined him. The wraith's shrieks increased and I began to hear the crackling of stone. I smiled as the sound intensified; the black stone that had sung for my life was disintegrating behind us.

The din was unbearable, waves of sound making both of us cringe. I felt a trembling in my hands soon matched by August's, a finality to it that was impossible to deny. My voice cracked in two when our blended powers whipped out, wrapping around the wraith, enveloping it in a blanket of energy.

Its screams mingled with the explosion of stone behind us. The blaze of light was blinding white, making us shut our eyes in its glare.

And then silence. So much of it, I thought I'd gone deaf.

"Anne, look."

I opened my eyes. Ash rained down on us, sprinkled with glittering, stone specks.

The moon was bright against the snow, making our two pale faces glow in the cold air. A seep of liquid splashed against my shoe and I looked up.

My gasp drew August's attention. Where the fountain had been was a huge puddle of dark liquid. It could be nothing else than blood.

August's hands fell away from my own and he attempted to stand. He hissed as his leg shifted position, his face blanching with the effort.

"Wait. Don't try to stand yet." I rose and saw the blood edging closer to where he was sitting, as if it was a living thing. I shuddered.

"On second thought, let's get away from this spot."

Casting my eyes about, I found a long stick, a branch that, though thin, was full of fibrous strength.

"Here, use this."

August forced it down into the snow and gripped it tightly with both hands. With a grunt, he lifted his good leg under him, allowing his body to turn as it wished, while his ravaged leg throbbed in limp agony.

He pressed his forehead against the branch, and I could see beads of clear sweat shining on his pale skin.

"August." I edged up to his hunched frame. "Do you think it's broken?"

He didn't look up, but nodded. "It threw me across the room, into a wall. I thought the wraith had broken my spine."

"It thought so, too."

He raised a hand to his head and a twist of pain knotted around his features as his fingers prodded the back of his skull. "I don't remember how I got here. Last thing I can recall is slamming against that wall. I'm afraid I must have hit my head at some point during this charming night."

I smiled at him.

"I don't remember much either after we—well, after you . . ."

My face was hot against the night air, and I thanked the Lord that it was still too dark for August to notice. I didn't wait for a response, but turned around to survey the splotched landscape we'd created.

"How did you know it was Lily?" August asked.

I swallowed the sudden lump of nerves in my throat. "She was in the manor."

I watched as he processed my words, his skin growing paler in the moonlight. "But the letter I received all those years ago—"

"She falsified her death so you wouldn't suspect she was the one tormenting you."

He took a deep breath. "She pretended to be dead for all these years, just to harm me?"

"Yes." I bit my lower lip. "She showed me what happened between the two of you."

He flinched. "Oh. Anne, I'm sorry. I should have told you."

I nodded. "Why didn't you?"

"I didn't want you to know I'd behaved so horribly. I was ashamed, the guilt of thinking everything I'd done had led her to her death was too much. But I should have told you when you asked. There is no excuse but my cowardice."

I shook my head. It didn't matter anymore, not really, not after everything. "Is it over now?"

"No. We banished the wraith, true, but as long as Lily is still alive, I don't know if it'll ever be over."

I knew those words should have frightened me, the realization that we'd only really bought ourselves some time, and that we'd have to face even more darkness in the future, but the exhaustion I felt was too great to focus on any of that. For now, at least, we were safe.

August suddenly shifted his body toward me, as if he'd just remembered something. "You were willing to try the entire chant."

He sounded as surprised as if he hadn't seen it with his own eyes minutes before.

"Pretty stupid, right?"

"Not the word I would have chosen, but yes. And dangerous."

August's breathing grew ragged and tight, the air whistling through his clenched lips as he inched toward me.

My blood scurried up and down my limbs in an exhausting race, awaiting the familiar warmth of his presence against my skin. I didn't turn around.

With a sigh, he pressed his lips against the back of my head, allowing my hair to dampen the burn.

"Thank you," he whispered.

I closed my eyes and nodded.

A thought flashed into my head. "Oh, August, the manor! The roses! They're destroyed!"

He shrugged and sighed. "It doesn't matter. Not anymore."

We moved slowly toward the manor, the smell sharp and biting, wood still shrieking as it collapsed to the ground, only to be devoured by the flames. August wavered at the sight of the burnt roses. He shook his head, as if to dislodge a lump of sadness.

"Let it burn to the ground."

We watched the fire for a long time, seeing it grow weaker as it ran out of things to destroy. My mind was too sore to think, so I allowed myself to just be, to just stand beside the puzzling man hunched next to me, to just feel the night in my hair. I suddenly felt something cold on my shoulder, seeping wet through my gown.

Snow. It was falling all over us. I smiled and looked at August, who turned his face toward it. The sound of sizzling reached us as the snow smothered the fire.

There was a sudden vibration from the ground. I turned to August in surprise.

His eyes sparkled like crystals in the moonlight, and as his smile widened, I began to see and hear green shooting up out of the trampled snow, thick stalks that grew and expanded, each carrying a red drop at its center. Gasping, I saw the red mold itself, turn, multiply. Bloom.

The perfume burst into the air in all its madness as I turned around. We were standing in a circle of roses.

I laughed and cast him a sideways glance.

"What now?"

He shrugged. "Anything we want."

"We?"

He looked at me with such warmth, I felt my cheeks reddening. "Of course, Anne." He held my gaze for a moment more, then cleared his throat and looked away. "You didn't think I'd part with the only Grounder I know, did you? Do you really expect me to snuff out my own candles? The horror."

For a second, I froze, contemplating his words. I didn't know what they meant, not really, but I decided I didn't care. Laughing, I shook my head.

August bent down with many grunts and winces and picked off one of the fragrant roses. Rising to his full height, he offered it to me with a soft smile.

"For a new beginning. For a new life."

ACKNOWLEDGEMENTS

It's been years since I first wrote this novel's first draft. Since then, a number of people have been crucial in getting it to you in the shape now hold and hopefully enjoyed. Although the story remains intrinsically similar to the one I first conceived, it is a better novel for all the people who have touched it since I jotted it down in my red Moleskine notebook.

My editor, **Kisa**, for your enthusiasm, your invaluable comments on the trickiest scenes, and for giving Lily the emotional girth she deserved.

Thank you, **Ashley**, for giving my novel a chance and for being so unbelievably helpful and kind to a first time author. It has been a privilege to work with REUTS Publications.

I want to also thank **Summer** and **Tiffany** who have done such an amazing job putting together all the promotional materials for the novel. You two really understood the "feel" of what I wanted and made it a reality.

Thank you also to my family, in particular my **sister**, who put up with my neurotic concerns and who allowed me to bounce ideas off her until one of them rung true.

And last but never least, thank you to **Loki** and **Carabosse**, for being constant creatures of joy around my laptop.

ABOUT THE AUTHOR

Valentina Cano is a student of classical singing who spends whatever free time she has either reading or writing. She also watches over a veritable army of pets, including her five, very spoiled, snakes. Her works have appeared in numerous publications and her poetry has been nominated for the Pushcart Prize and Best of the Web. She lives in Miami, Florida.

www.ingramcontent.com/pod-product-compliance
Lightning Source LLC
Chambersburg PA
CBHW030224180626
46810CB00008B/2948